PATH
to
My African Eyes

Ermila Moodley

Just Us Books, Inc.
East Orange, NJ
www.justusbooks.com

PATH TO MY AFRICAN EYES

Published by Just Us Books, Inc.
ISBN 978-1-933491-09-7

For information regarding permission, write to:

Just Us Books, Inc.

356 Glenwood Avenue,

East Orange, NJ 07017

www.justusbooks.com

Library of Congress Cataloging-in-Publication Data is available

10 9 8 7 6 5 4 3 2

Printed in China

Jacket design by Chuck Yuen

Photograph by 2nd Chapter

For my mother

Chapter 1

*Y*esterday I looked perfect. Dressed in low-rise Guess jeans, blue V-neck, and cropped denim jacket with the sewn-on "Question Authority" patch, I looked like the models in *Today's Teen*. That is if you ignored my shortly-cropped kinky hair and chestnut skin. I felt confident I could waltz into my first day at Buena Vista High looking like I owned the world.

But on this nail-biting Monday morning, the mirror seems to have gutted my image. I cringe at the fake in front of me. The entire freshman class is going to see right through my act. I just know it. I crunch my knuckles, picturing their cross-eyed looks.

Tearing off the outfit that seemed so right less than twenty four hours ago, I feverishly hunt through my closet for something more understated. Something that smacks of impeccable taste, yet gives the impression it was just grabbed out of the closet. I consider my favorite green Table Mountain sweatshirt. No, too souvenir shop. My purple mohair sweater catches my eye. I love its soft, silky feel. I slip it on but as I examine my reflection, my heart sinks. Purple is not this winter's color. That was made very clear in the fashion magazine I scrutinized yesterday.

"Thandi! Thandi!" Mum calls from the kitchen. "Hurry up, or you'll be late."

I frantically rifle through the clothes in my closet. But nothing, absolutely nothing, seems right for this important occasion. I was never been big on fashion and clothes before moving here. In Cape Town, school uniforms and a fixation on academics dampened those kinds of interests. My best friend, Stacy, always said, "Thandi, face it, you have no fashion sense."

But in Buena Vista, California, where kids drive their own sports cars and vacation in Hawaii for spring break, plain Jane just won't do. I plan to embrace a whole new, trendy me. I'm determined to totally fit into my new world.

In my closet I uncover a beige scarf. It's just the thing to complement my outfit, giving me the hint of chicness that I need. So, I wriggle back into the blue V-neck, wrap the silky scarf loosely around my neck, throw on the denim jacket, and dash to the kitchen, where Mum is slicing tomatoes while listening to the news on the radio.

A bowl of sand-colored rings mocks me from the breakfast table. I eyeball it, while trying to still all the different feelings swimming inside me. I push a few rings into my reluctant mouth. "Not hungry, Mum," I grunt and drink my orange juice.

Mum puts the knife down and shakes the

cereal box at me. "*Cheerios*, Thandi. Dad's friend told us American kids love it. Just try it, at least." She hates sending me off to school with an empty belly. Something to do with her poverty-stricken childhood days in rural South Africa.

I force a few more tasteless rings down my throat. Mum grins, eyeing me from head to toe, as she zips my lunch bag. I know she's dying to say something about the way I'm dressed but is exercising restraint. Then she squeezes my shoulders and says, "All these firsts you're going to experience today, Thandi. Ooh mama, *yebo*, you must be nervous."

"Freshman year at an American high school," I murmur. "I can't believe it's actually happening." My stomach aches with tension. Today I'll be starting a new grade in a new country. And as if that's not bad enough, it's January, the middle of the school year.

"Morning, morning," Dad sings as he waltzes into the kitchen. He stops abruptly and jerks his head back. "Thandi, what're … where's your uniform?"

My dear old-fashioned, too-wrapped-up-in-academics dad. I sigh dramatically. "Dad, hel-lo-oh!" He pours himself some coffee, inhaling deeply. "Can't beat the smell of dark roasted beans," he mutters with a smile of satisfaction.

Morning rituals over, Mum, Dad, and I file out of the kitchen and into our newly purchased car, a Volvo station wagon. We're off to my school, Buena Vista High. I sit at the edge of the back seat cracking each of my knuckles.

Mum switches on the demister and the foggy windows begin to clear up. "Feels so strange for it to be winter in January," she comments.

I exhale loudly to release some tension. "I wish we could've moved in September."

"Blame UCT's stubbornness," Dad says. He had to complete the academic year at the University of Cape Town before he could start his new job as a professor here. The school year in South Africa starts in February and ends in December, which is why we arrived in Buena Vista a few days after Christmas and smack dab in the middle of the school year. Back in Cape Town, I'd be enjoying summer break.

Dad swerves into the school parking lot and hits a bump hard, causing us to jerk forward. He's not the world's best driver. He gives me an affectionate thump on my shoulder as I jump out. "Don't worry, Thandi. You'll blend right in. Isn't that what the principal said?"

I smile, grab my backpack, ease out of the car and wave goodbye to my parents. Last Friday I took a placement test at Buena Vista High. When Mum and I met with the principal later that day, she seemed thoroughly impressed at the high level and advanced concepts I had already mastered. Mum explained that the private school I went to, Siyafunda, was the most elite in South Africa, preparing their students for the best universities in the world. "You should have no trouble starting ninth grade this late in the year," the principal, Ms. Moore, assured me. "Have you turned fourteen yet?"

I nodded. "Last month."

"Good. You'll blend right in." And so, even though I completed eighth grade only a month ago, I'm about to start ninth grade halfway through the year. That prospect scares the heck out of me, but I swallow my panic and glance at my schedule for the day as I head toward the office.

First period is English. At the front office I pick up a campus map. Ms. Moore sees me and comes over. She's a large woman with ginger colored hair that's pulled into a severe bun. She smiles at me warmly, exposing big, coffee-stained teeth. "Thandi, I told my kids we have a new student from South Africa. They were very excited. They can't wait to meet you."

I open my mouth to ask why, but my courage fails me. Her height and loudness are intimidating.

"Well, have a great first day," Ms. Moore says with a dismissive smile. My heart hammering, I seek out my first class.

First period bell has already rung by the time I find the classroom. As I turn the doorknob I get a sudden urge to run away. It all feels so huge, so impersonal. I crave the familiarity of my old school, Siyafunda. I'd gone there since kindergarten. It was like my second home.

Silence greets me when I enter the classroom. An assortment of perfumes hang in the air. My cheeks warm as Mrs. Stevens, the English teacher, looks up with a motherly smile. Her face is crisscrossed with lines like aged leather. Her walnut eyes shine with alertness. It's obvious she is expecting me.

"Thandi Sobuh-kwee?"

I nod, stifling an urge to correct her pronunciation of my name. She turns to the class and introduces me. "Class, this is Thandi Sobuh-kwee. She's new to the school. New to California, in fact. She's just moved here from South Africa." Her high-pitched voice exudes a friendly energy.

The students' curious stares bore through me. I've never felt so self-conscious before. What could they be thinking?

Mrs. Stevens throws a slender arm around me, maneuvering me to a desk in the middle of the room. I sit down, then take in my surroundings, amazed at how different everything is from my Cape Town school. The most noticeable thing is the way everyone is dressed. Casual jeans and light sweaters make for a laid-back atmosphere. Contrast that with our formal uniforms at Siyafunda. Our classrooms reeked of discipline. A survey of the girls tells me I'm overdressed. I slowly pull off my scarf and shove it into my pocket.

The newness and strangeness of the class make it hard for me to focus on the chapter Mrs. Stevens assigned us to read silently. I notice the absence of other Black kids in the class. Not a surprise to me. A week ago one of Dad's new colleagues, a professor who grew up in Venezuela, told us over dinner that there were very few Black families in Buena Vista. "California is strange that way," he said. "Most Black people live in L.A. or Oakland." Dad and Mum expressed disappointment. I felt neutral. In Cape Town, I was as close to my White friends as to my Black friends.

A long time passes before I become aware of Mrs. Stevens again. She passes out a worksheet and says, "Because it's the first week after winter break, I've selected a simple vocabulary list for the week. We'll be looking at words with Greek roots." A glance at the list of familiar words blots out some of my tension.

Then I sense someone's eyes on me. I look up and notice a round-faced boy who quickly turns his head away. His blond hair is parted and pressed down neatly. Dressed in a long-sleeved, white-collared shirt and a blue and black striped vest, he looks like a private school student. His appearance arouses my curiosity.

The bell rings as we come to the end of the vocabulary list. Mrs. Stevens shouts out a reminder over an eruption of noise. "Don't forget your homework is to write a literary response to the chapter we read today." We trundle out into the breezy hall. I button up my jacket.

I'm poring over the map to see where my next class is when I hear someone clearing his or her throat. An odd pair of boys, one several inches taller than me, the other a runt, stand in front of me staring rudely into my face. I recognize them from my English class. The tall, curly haired one with acne on his huge nose, screws up his face as if deeply puzzled. "Male or female? Girl or boy?" he asks me.

A spurt of anger instantly grips me. My body stiffens. It takes all my willpower to keep me from smacking him across his smug face. I glare at the ridiculous pair, then turn back to the map. In a daze, I locate my second period class—Algebra, and race down the hall. *Calm down*, I tell myself, trying not to gouge my palms with my nails.

The teacher, a tall, dark-haired man named Mr. Wilson, begins a lesson on algebraic equations when I enter the room. I glance around, and with immense relief notice that those two slugs aren't in this class. I take a seat in the first empty chair I spot, which is right behind a lanky boy with bony shoulders.

I take a good look at each kid while Mr. Wilson works out equations. Girl. Girl. Boy. Boy. Girl. Boy. Girl. Girl. Girl. Boy. My heart sinks lower and lower. Even the girls with flat chests who are dressed like boys are unmistakably girls.

It's my hair. My annoyingly short and kinky hair that makes me look like a boy. While practically all Black girls in Cape Town have straightened hair or extensions, my mum is adamant about me maintaining the natural look. It's a political thing with her and a frustrating source of conflict between us.

The absence of Black kids in this class fills me with an unexpected sense of loneliness. I would never have guessed I'd feel this way. At Siyafunda, of the twenty students in my eighth grade class, six were Black and the rest were White. Apart from the arrogant Richard Hoffman and downright rude David Van Niekerk, I felt as comfortable with my White classmates as I did with my Black ones. Richard and David talked down to me. They'd say things like, "Have you heard of Shakespeare?" or "Do you even understand that there's a difference between philosophy and psychology?"

Jerks! Their ignorance never bothered me, though. Everyone hated them, making them great fodder for jokes. I loved all my other classmates. Since we were private school brats, we all had middle class, well-educated parents. So our home lives were similar and race didn't seem to play a role, at least not in any way I could see.

"Thandi?"

I look up, startled out of my daydreaming.

"You're from Africa?" Mr. Wilson asks as he hands me a worksheet. His brown sweater is stretched and lifted up at the bottom by his large belly.

"*South* Africa."

"What country?" His large forehead creases into rows of parallel lines.

I frown, not for the first time feeling the letdown that comes when you realize your teachers don't know everything. "South Africa."

He nods and moves on.

My neighbor tilts her freckled face toward me. "My grandma went to Africa last year. She went on, like a safari. Says Africa's a beautiful country." She smiles like a bank clerk, as if she's just paid me a compliment.

"Continent. Africa is a continent," I tell her.

She nods, a foolish look clouding her face. She squints at her worksheet, then turns back to me. "I'm Erin, by the way. And you're - Thandi. Am I pronouncing it right?"

I nod. "Yup. Rhymes with candy."

We get to work on our math assignment. I sail through the equations, thankful that we covered this at Siyafunda. So far I'm blending in academically just as Ms. Moore promised.

Between classes, I take a break outside. As I munch on a carrot stick at a picnic table in the snack area, I notice a long-legged Black girl marching toward my table. A gold stud glints from her nose, and multiple earrings decorate her small ears. She smiles and waves in my direction. I smile and just as I raise my hand to wave back, I realize that she's heading toward a couple of students behind me. Feeling foolish, I lower my head and fumble with the zipper of my backpack.

I try to make eye contact with the Black girl and her friends, but they seem completely wrapped up in some story. I turn enviously to other clusters of students, wishing I were in a cluster too.

As I make my way to World History class, someone bumps into my shoulder. It's the big-nosed slug and his friend. "Sausage lips," he mutters.

His runtish friend doubles over, then says, "Midnight." They punch each other's fists and swagger into the classroom.

Stunned, I blink at the ground. Did that really

happen? I shake my head in disbelief, then walk into the room with my head bowed. The presence of the two slugs in this room makes it impossible to concentrate on Ancient China.

I feel riled up in a way that Richard and David could never succeed in doing. And I don't know why. Both groups of guys were picking on me, but somehow, the slugs' taunting felt different.

I look at my hands. Dark brown, with darker areas by the knuckles. I examine my fingers. I can see the distinct lines where the pink skin of my palm meets the back of my fingers. I look at the teacher's hands. No lines. His palms and the backs of his hands blend seamlessly. I look at my arms. The color of dark chocolate. I look at my neighbor's arms. I'm reminded of the light pink rose petals I loved to sniff in our old garden. Uncomfortably aware of myself, I force myself to pay attention to the Ming Dynasty lesson.

◊◊◊◊◊

Mum and Dad are waiting in the car in the school parking lot when school lets out. "So, how was it?" Dad asks. He smiles briefly, then knits his brows as he starts up the car. I can tell that my first day at school is not the biggest thing on his mind.

I fake a cheerful smile. "Good."

"I bet it was very different from Siyafunda," Mum says. She presses my shoulder tenderly.

"Uh-huh. Yeah. Seems a lot easier."

"What about friends? Made any yet?" Mum asks.

"No, but I'm sure I will. Everyone was really nice and friendly. Well, except for a few immature idiots." My voice gets unsteady. Something stops me from telling them about the ugly episode with the two boys. I guess it's because I can't do what Mum and Dad would expect me to do—just shrug it off. "World's full of jerks," Dad is famous for stating.

I, however, feel pretty mixed up about the teasing today. After all the agony of preparing for this first day to go just right, how could it have gone so wrong? I crack my knuckles and frown. Something inside me has been dislodged. I'm dreading my second day at Buena Vista High.

Chapter
2

Girl or boy? That stinging question takes hold of me as I weave my way through the noisy tables in the school cafeteria. Why did it hurt so much yesterday when those idiots asked me that? Was it because of the hateful way they said it? How would I feel if someone asked me that question more innocently? Embarrassed? Yes. Hurt? Don't know.

It's lunchtime, and I plant myself beside Jennifer Sullivan, a girl who is in most of my classes. I am not shy, nor particularly patient, and I'm not going to delay the process of making friends. I pinned down Jennifer as a candidate because of her vivaciousness, a quality you see in her instantly. I've always been drawn to people like her—extroverts who ooze self-confidence. I guess that's how I'd like to be, too. I watch her now, laughing her head off, commanding the attention of everyone at her table.

"Hello. My name is Thandi. But I guess you

already know that," I say, with a nervous giggle. I take in her fitted, low-rise jeans studded with beads and metal stars.

"Hi, Thandi. What d'ya have for lunch?" Jennifer asks, tossing her silky hair.

I glance at my sandwich. "A cheese and tomato sandwich." Everyone around me bursts out laughing. I cringe. Did I say something stupid? Or is it because I brought a lunch from home? Everyone else seems to be eating something from the school cafeteria.

Then a short girl, with her brown hair in a ponytail, says, mocking me, "A cheese and to-mah-to sandwich." A mouthful of braces burdens her with a lisp. Thank heavens my braces came off before we left Cape Town. But no one seems to care how she talks. They all laugh at me. My face gets hot. I rub off the sweat below my nose.

Jennifer frowns at the girl. "Chrystal, that happens to be her accent." Then turning to me with a smile, she says, "I love the way you talk. It sounds so British."

"Thanks." I actually can't wait to lose my South African accent to a swanky American one.

After lunch, Jennifer, Chrystal, and I stroll out toward the basketball court. "The cutest sophomore boys are playing basketball," Jennifer gushes. "Want to come watch?" Her voice is melodic.

"Sure." A rush of excitement shoots through me at the invitation.

As we approach the game, Jennifer starts cheering and pumping her fists in the air. "Go, Ryan!"

Chrystal, mellow, with a voice to match, winks at me. "All the girls are hot for Ryan. Take a look at that bod'! Solid muscle." She points to a boy who is about to shoot the ball. He looks like a normal White boy to me. I can't see what the fuss is all about. Well, okay, he is very tall. So tall that he just dunks the ball through the hoop effortlessly.

Jennifer nudges me in the side. "Is he cool, or what!"

"He is," I respond. I notice two of the players are Black. I watch them weave through the other players in pursuit of the ball.

"Hey, Thandi To-mah-to, d'you play basketball in Africa?" Chrystal asks. In her grey long-sleeved T-shirt and plain jeans, she lacks Jennifer's glamour.

"You mean, *South* Africa," I say, irritably. And what's with that dumb teasing name? "Africa is a big continent and I'm from one of its countries."

Jennifer and Chrystal roll their eyes as if to say, "Drop the geography lesson!"

"Sorry. No, there's no basketball in South Africa."

"You're kidding," Jennifer says dramatically. "What about baseball and football?"

I shake my head.

She cocks her head at me, blue eyes wide with astonishment. Her wheat-colored hair falls to one shoulder. "It must be so boring not to have sports like we do."

I frown defensively at her. "We have our own sports."

"Dodging the animals?" Chrystal quips, smirking.

My eyes pop open in surprise. I'm just about to defend my country by telling them about soccer and rugby, when I hear a cough. I automatically turn to a strapping girl with spiky hair, wearing beige shorts and a fleece jacket. Her green eyes bore into my skull. I smile at her. Her blank expression doesn't change. She just continues her silent staring.

I know it can't be my newly-purchased slim fit jeans and green turtleneck. Quite a few other girls have on similar clothes. Could it be my shoes? I glance at my white Nike sneakers. Most of the others are wearing black boots. But this girl's eyes are on my face. I feel hot and sweaty despite the chill in the air. I cast my head down, and crack my knuckles.

A tug on my shoulder pulls my attention. It's Jennifer. "Thandi, meet Tess, star tennis player, heading for the U.S. Open." I turn and look into the smiling face of a girl I recognize from Algebra class. She has a big beauty spot on her right cheek.

"Thandi's from Africa," Jennifer says, continuing her introduction.

Tess's eyes widen, and her mouth falls open. "Africa?" She rolls out the word, looking curiously at me while this information sinks in. She takes a deep breath and turns to Jennifer. "Does she speak English?"

My jaw drops and I'm ready to punch her face.

"Of course she speaks English, Tess. Jeez!"

"What's it like there?" she asks, speaking

directly to me this time. "Do they have cars and television and stuff?"

I can't tell if that's a serious question, so I decide to ignore it. The 'starer' girl in beige shorts merges with us and joins in the conversation. "Is it true that in Africa people don't have bathrooms?" Her face still shows no expression making me wonder if she has the ability to move any facial muscles other than those that control her lips.

The other girls squeal with laughter. One of them says, "Oh yeah, an aunt of mine went to Africa last year. And she said she and the people in her tour group were worried about getting sick. She said there weren't any proper doctors in Africa and if they needed a doctor they would have to fly to Europe." Everyone turns to me, expecting verification of this ridiculous statement.

What are they thinking? That my home is a jungle? And what is this "Africa" business? Do they think the whole continent is the same all over? Their ignorance astounds me.

I wish I could just look them in the eye and say, "You're all a bunch of idiots!" But courage right now, or lack of it, is only part of the problem. What I'm most aware of is a deep shame creeping through me. I visualize Kheima, a Xhosa village, where my grandmother lives. I call this place "the other world." My grandmother lives in a nice brick house that my parents had built for her. But most of her neighbors and the other villagers live in mud huts and have outhouse toilets. I picture the cows and chickens running around in their yards, and the outside fire where they cook their food. The tribal world, though not even close to how I lived in Cape Town, is home to many South Africans. This reality I find very embarrassing.

I escape from the group by telling them I have to use the restroom. I wander off feeling like a burst balloon. The two slugs from yesterday notice me and deliberately walk toward me. I know their names now. Nathan, a.k.a. Nate, is the runt. Big Nose is Matthew, a.k.a. Matt. I change course and head for my locker. They don't follow.

As I get out my books for sixth period I imagine how easy life must be for girls with beautiful, blue eyes and blond hair that blows in the wind.

◊◊◊◊◊

The next morning I awaken to a bright, sunny day. The house feels amazingly warm, even though the heating hasn't been turned on. When I step out of the shower, Mum says, "The weatherman says it's going to be eighty degrees today. Can you believe it? And tomorrow it's supposed to be even warmer! And this is the middle of winter!"

So I wear shorts and a T-shirt to school.

As I amble into first period class, Jennifer, in shorts and a tank top, strides up to me. "Hey, Thandi, wanna go with me and Chrystal to the beach tomorrow afternoon? We're going to Paradise Beach. This hot weather we're having, it's very unusual. My mom says we should make the most of it." Her genuine interest in me excites me. It makes me feel welcome in my new school.

"Sure, love to. Actually, my house is close to Paradise. I can walk there."

"D'you have a boogie board?" Jennifer asks. I shake my head. I don't even know how to use one.

"Oh, that's okay," she bubbles on. "We'll be taking ours."

I turn around and notice the shirt-and-vest starer doing his annoying thing again. I've lost count of how many times I've caught him looking at me. I ask Jennifer who he is.

She pulls me close to her and whispers, "Mr. Britannica. His real name is Peter. Really, really smart, but"—she grimaces, pauses, then points her index finger to her temple and rotates it—"whacko! Deck's missing a few cards."

Mrs. Stevens says, "Quiet class. Settle down. Time for an expository writing activity." On the board she writes:

AN EXTRAORDINARY INVENTION

Mrs. Stevens explains that we have to write a few paragraphs about an invention that is not only useful, but also shows innovative thinking. She moves in slow motion today, her voice sounding thick, as if she had a late night. The class obliges her and gets quiet.

As for me, my head buzzes with confusing thoughts about all the different encounters I've had at Buena Vista High. I feel like I'm on one of those strange roller coaster rides—one moment going sideways, and the next moment jolted upward.

Normally, writing about a topic like this would

be a cinch. Science is right up my alley. With a dad intent on stuffing my brain with all it can handle, and a natural love and aptitude for the field, developing an invention would normally thrill me to bits. But getting my brain to behave right now proves to be a challenge. I keep thinking about Nate and Matt.

"About five minutes left to finish up those essays," Mrs. Stevens says.

I look down at my paper. The only thing I've written is my name. I've got to come up with something. My eyes dance around the classroom. I notice Chrystal and Jennifer using a sort of sign language to talk to each other. An idea that I thought about some time ago floats back into my mind. I grab my pencil and scribble:

Thandi's Telepen

One of the most frustrating things in class is when you are dying to tell your friend something and you can't because you're not allowed to talk. Well, scientists thrive on solving problems, so I decided this was a problem I would take on to demonstrate my scientific mind.

I tried to think of all the ways people communicate with each other: radio, telephone, notes, speaking, e-mail, instant messaging. I realized if we combine the principles of two or more of these methods, we could create just the right device. Of course, if cell phones were allowed on campus we could send text messages to our friends. That would be the easiest solution. So how about if we used the same idea but with different technology in a way that camouflaged what we were doing? What if we used a pair of special pens that could 'talk' to each other? Friends would be able to communicate anywhere on campus, within the classroom, while in different classes, or wherever they are. This device would work by radio transmission, making them far more affordable than cell phones.

This is how I came to invent Thandi's TelePen. This device comes in pairs. Each pen has a small screen and a little keypad. But other than that, they look pretty much like normal pens, just broader. They are noiseless and easy to keep in your pocket. When you wish to send a message, you press keys with a pencil tip, and the other pen picks up the message, producing a vibration while it does. The receiver can then read and respond. It took some hard work to create this gadget, but it turned out to be a roaring success.

I read over the essay and fall into a daydream. I become famous because of this miraculous pen. Oblivious to my physical appearance, everyone treats me like royalty.

Chapter 3

*I*t's my fourth day at Buena Vista High. I still feel the same amount of tension as on my first day. I approach my desk in first period and notice a neatly wrapped cookie on it. A little note is taped to the wrapper.

> *Dear Thandi (or is it Thandie?),*
> *I helped Dad make chocolate chip cookies*
> *last night. Hope you like it.*
>
> *Your friend, Peter.*

Your friend, Peter? Mr. Britannica, the starer, thinks he is my friend? Oh, no. No, no, no. I am absolutely *not* going to be friends with some geek that nobody likes. Especially someone Jennifer dislikes. As I settle down, I'm aware of Peter's eyes on me. I carefully keep my focus on the front of the room.

Mrs. Stevens picks up a stack of papers and sits on her stool at the front of the classroom. "Some of you have written excellent expository essays. But the one I found most impressive was the one written by our new student who must be a budding scientist." She smiles warmly at me, her face carved into deep creases. "Thandi, may I read your essay to the class?"

My mouth falls open. I don't know what to say. I mean, of course I'm flattered at her compliment, especially as I'm new to ninth grade. But what would my classmates think? Flustered, I pull my shoulders up in a small shrug.

She takes this to mean yes and begins to read. I feel myself breaking into a sweat and fasten my eyes on my desk. When she's finished, the class remains quiet. No smirks or wisecracks. I breathe a sigh of relief.

Mrs. Stevens hands me my paper, commenting, "Let's hope I'm retired when kids enter the radio pen era."

Before my next class I go to my locker to get a snack. As soon as I get the combination lock open, I hear a voice. I spin around and find my eyes meeting a pair of watery, grayish-blue eyes. Peter smiles at me shyly and winks. I look up to see if anyone noticed, then ignoring him, I walk briskly away.

On the way, I pass a pair of students from English class. "Cool invention," one of them says. A charming smile enhances his movie-star looks.

"If you have any available, I want one," the

other guy, massively overweight, says. "It's great to have someone with imagination at our school."

"Thanks." I flash a smile of gratitude at them.

As I navigate my way to a bench under The Big Tree, our school's famous oak, the Black girl with the pierced nose walks past me. More accurately, she glides past me, head held high, a cocky expression on her face. A skinny girl with henna-dyed hair glides alongside her. I clear my throat and call out, "Hi."

Both girls stop and turn around. "A new sista at our school," the Black girl says. *Sis-tuh.* That's how she pronounces it. "Where you from?"

"South Africa. Cape Town. I'm Thandi."

"I'm Ciara, and this is Lynn." Ciara has an accent that seems to be common among the Black folks in Southern California—just short of a southern drawl. Coming from a country that borrows most of its popular culture from the U.S., I'm familiar with all the different American accents.

"We have media studies way over there. Gotta run." They wave good-bye.

I smile to myself as I munch Peter's cookie. I'm a *sista*.

Peter's cookie is unbelievably delicious, filling me with guilt. How can I tell him we can't be friends? That he would be totally detrimental to the image I'm trying to cultivate?

The bell rings for fourth period. Time for Spanish, which, so far, is my favorite class. What fun it is to learn expressions in a new language. Spanish seems to be as common in Buena Vista as English.

Everywhere we go we hear people speaking Spanish. But so far, at Buena Vista, I've seen only a handful of Spanish-speaking students.

I love the teacher, Mr. Garcia. He is charming, not to mention young and handsome. He lacks classroom control though.

I'm just about to plop on my seat in Spanish class when I notice a note on my desk. Oh no, not Mr. Britannica, again. But this time the paper is wrinkled and scruffy. I open it and slide onto my chair. The words that blast out at me make the blood drain from my head.

"GO BACK TO AFRICA, SAUSAGE LIPS."

I look up to see if anyone saw me reading the note. The students all seem absorbed in finishing yesterday's homework.

I inhale deeply and try to stop trembling. I force myself to focus on Mr. Garcia. I feel as if I've shrunk to the size of an ant.

What should I do about the note? I contemplate showing it to Mr. Garcia, but I decide against it. I can't bear the embarrassment of him knowing the teasing name they have for me.

Why can't those slugs leave me alone?

◊◊◊◊◊

A final bell announces the end of the school day. I head to the park where Mum runs laps for her daily exercise. Mum is a food and health reporter for a weekly magazine based in Cape Town. Because she sits in front of her computer all morning, she feels the need to get out for fresh air and sunshine in the afternoon. She times herself to finish her running when I'm through with school so we can walk home together. I cross over to where Mum is doing stretches under a huge sycamore. As we stroll up the block to our house, she asks, "How was school today, darling?"

My heart stops. Can she tell it was horrible beyond words? I'm not going to tell her about the note. I can't bear to think about it, let alone talk about it.

"Fine," I say, faking lightheartedness. "I met a sista."

Her lips curve into an amused smile.

"Her name's Ciara."

"That's wonderful. Hope you become friends."

"Oh, and someone brought me a chocolate chip cookie."

"A chocolate chip cookie! *Ooh mama*! How was it?" Mum and I have a terrible weakness for home-baked goodies. It's the only unhealthy food we indulge in.

"Mmmm, no offense, Mum, but it was the tastiest cookie I've ever had," I say, smacking my lips. Then a wave of guilt comes over me. I wasn't nice to Peter. I didn't even thank him. That boy is such a puzzle. Why would he think he is my friend?

"But the best thing about today is still to

happen. My new friends are going to teach me to boogie board."

Mum chuckles. "I'm glad you're a good swimmer. So, think you're going to like Buena Vista?"

"I don't know, Mum," I mumble, my mood turning bleak as I think about the note.

She is quick to sense that something is on my mind. "Thandi, out with it. What's the problem?"

I take a deep breath and let out a sigh. I can't bring myself to tell her about The Slugs. I notice an orange and black butterfly gliding in front of me. I've never seen those colors on a butterfly before. It dips down and settles on a plant. I run ahead to get a closer look. Mum catches up.

"I bought you a diary, today, Thandi. California is going to be a great experience for us. I really think you should keep a diary."

I groan. This is not the first time she's tried to make me do this. But, unlike my journalist mother, writing is not my idea of fun.

Mum puts an arm around me and pulls a sleek little leather book from her waist pouch. "Look, it's not easy starting out in a new place, especially at your age. A diary can help you through the rough patches. There'll be lots of challenges. I know. Trust me, I know."

She knows? What does she know? I fire her a mean look. The anger comes from The Slugs, but I take it out on her.

"You know?" I scream. "You know? How could you know? You and Dad are out of touch!" I stomp ahead of her so she wouldn't see my tears.

◊◊◊◊◊

When we get home, Mum and I both ignore my outburst and snack on strawberries and a creamy yogurt—a treat we discovered we are both addicted to. Then I shove a towel and a change of clothes into a bag, and jaunt down the path to Paradise Beach. Excitement about my first beach outing with my new friends lifts my spirits.

I spot them when I hear Chrystal yelling, "Thandi To-mah-to! Over here!"

Is she ever going to stop that teasing?

Jennifer and Chrystal, in Polynesian-patterned two-piece bathing suits, wave to me from a cozy corner against the wall of the cliff. I'm a little taken aback at their revealing suits. I've only ever owned one-piece suits.

With Chrystal and Jennifer are two women and a little girl. "Thandi, this is my mom, Anne," Jennifer says. Anne? I'm shocked that Jennifer introduces her mother by her first name. I can't imagine addressing an adult so casually.

Jennifer puts her arms around a beautiful woman whose face is a replica of hers, only older. Her mom is slender and dressed in snug shorts and a sleeveless shirt. She extends her hand to me. "Nice to meet you, Thandi." Her hand feels surprisingly cold.

She smells of aromatherapy lotion.

"This is my stepmom, Linda," chirps Chrystal, pointing to a woman whose bulging leg and arm muscles make her look like an athlete. "And this is my little sister, Chloe. Say hi to Thandi, Chloe."

Chloe, bright-eyed, with a head full of pretty curls, smiles shyly and creeps closer to me. "Hi," she says.

Linda gets out a little plastic bottle and says, "Let's get some sunscreen on you girls before you run off into the water. This sun will burn you in no time." Everyone takes a turn squeezing out some sunscreen, and the smell of apricots fills the air. Linda then hands the bottle to me. "Here, Thandi."

"No, thanks. I don't need it."

Jennifer turns to me with a puzzled look. "Don't you get sunburn?"

I shake my head. "I don't think so." Now I can feel everyone's eyes on me. My face gets hot.

"You mean, you can be in the sun a long time and nothing will happen to your skin?" Chrystal asks in disbelief.

I smile stupidly, as I pull my shoulders up in a small shrug. I wish they would shut up about my skin.

"So Thandi, what's it like in Africa?" Anne asks.

I stifle a groan as a picture of the whole continent flashes in front of me. A huge continent that, frankly, I know little about. We didn't do any traveling outside of Cape Town, except when we used to visit my Xhosa grandma in "the other world."

"I don't know," I say, deciding to take the question literally. "I'm from the part that's right at the bottom of the continent and it's the only part I know about."

I get confused looks from everyone, then nods and smiles. Chloe bursts into giggles and runs into my arms. I comb my fingers through her soft mass of light brown curls. They are the exact same brown as her saucer-shaped eyes.

"Take me to the water." She flutters her eyelashes at me.

"Sure." I turn to Chrystal and Jennifer. "I'll join you guys just now."

Chrystal tilts her head at me. "Just now? You mean soon?"

"Uh-huh." I nod, realizing once again that I used a uniquely South African expression. On my first day at school, I learned that my sneakers were not called takkies. And yesterday I learned that traffic lights are not called robots.

Chrystal reaches for her boogie board. "Jennifer Jellyfish, ready for some boogie boarding?"

"You betcha." Jennifer jumps up. So Jennifer has a teasing name too. Maybe this is one of Chrystal's quirks, not to be taken seriously.

"Oh, just a moment, girls." Linda jumps up from the sand, dusts herself off, and pulls a camera from a bulky leather bag. "I need to use up this film." She starts clicking away without waiting for anyone to pose. "Be natural," she murmurs. She handles the camera like a professional.

Chloe attaches herself to me like a mussel to a rock. It's fine with me because she's so cute. I've always wanted a little sister and this time with her is like scratching an itch. We splash around in the water, pretending to be dolphins. Swimming in the Pacific Ocean is fabulous, once you get over the shock of how cold the water is.

"Hey, Tanny, let's build a sand castle," Chloe suggests.

"Okay, we need to find a nice sandy spot."

Chloe and I are quiet as we create a nice, big bump. The warm sun feels wonderful on my skin. I inhale the salty air as we pat the sand into walls. Chloe suddenly stops and frowns at my hand. Then she looks up and says, "Tanny, Tanny, are you Black people?"

My heart lurches.

It's an innocent question from an innocent child. Yet for some reason, I feel like I've been stung by the snap of a rubber band. I don't say anything.

She repeats her question louder. "Tanny, are you Black people?"

"Uh-huh," I say, pretending to be concentrating on the sand castle. Satisfied with my answer, Chloe refocuses on our creation.

I want to run away and be alone. But before I can think of an excuse to leave, Jennifer and Chrystal shout and beckon for me to join them in the water.

"Come on, Thandi, we wanna show you how to

boogie board," they yell. When I join them, Jennifer hands me her boogie board and Chrystal demonstrates how to use it. I lay my body onto it but instantly roll off and fall into the water.

The girls giggle. "You have to paddle with your arms and legs once your body is on the board," Chrystal explains. I try again, and this time I glide smoothly over the gentle waves. It feels sensational.

"Time to go, girls," Anne calls out too soon.

Chrystal and Jennifer wrap their arms around my waist as we head back to where their mothers are waiting. We try to walk in a rhythm. First, we extend our left legs all at the same time, then our right legs. I picture a zebra with its alternating black and white stripes. A warmth blankets me. I've got friends who seem to like me.

Jennifer says, "You're cool, Thandi. You can come boogie boarding with us whenever we go. You'll need a wetsuit, though. Today, the weather is totally unusual, but on normal days, it's really cold in the water."

"Hey, Thandi, do you want to learn to surf?" Chrystal asks. She stops and looks at me with interest.

"Oh, right," Jennifer says, twirling around on her toes. "I'm about to inherit my brother's surfboard and Chrystal's going to give me lessons. You can join us too if you get a surfboard."

I'd never thought about surfing before, but the idea thrills me. I can't imagine anything more cool, more perfect for my new image, than riding the waves in the Pacific Ocean.

"Sure, I'd love that."

"Hang with us, girl, and we'll turn you into a true California babe," Chrystal says. She folds her arms and tilts her pointy chin at me, nodding slowly as if sizing up my potential.

I grin at my new friends with starry eyes. I know all about California babes. In South Africa most of our movies and television programs come from the U.S. So do our music and fashion. Many South Africans worship everything American. I picture the sexy Sara from the sitcom "Santa Monica," who loves to surf. And the voluptuous Korean-American, Grace, from the morning fitness show, "Health is Beauty," demonstrating yoga near the beach in Santa Barbara. My heart does joyful flips at the thought of becoming a California babe.

"Critical Chrystal. That's it. That's your nickname," I say, nudging her in the ribs.

To my surprise, Chrystal smiles in response. "Hey, to have a critical eye is a virtue. I like the sound of that. Thandi To-mah-to, Jennifer Jellyfish, and Critical Chrystal."

As I stroll home, my high spirits evaporate and an emptiness descends on me. I don't understand why my heart has stopped singing. Then the answer whacks me like a shower of pebbles. The girl in beige shorts staring at me as if I were from another planet. Tess and the others thinking I come from the jungle. Chrystal and Jennifer looking curiously at my skin that doesn't burn in the sun. And the biggest pebble. Those hateful slugs. A pain shoots through my stomach where the wound, raw and naked, lies.

Chloe's question about whether I'm "Black people" returns to my mind. Why did that affect me? I grapple with this until an answer comes. Maybe it reminded me that my skin color makes me different. And maybe I don't want to be defined by my skin color.

Chapter
4

*M*um and Dad are in the middle of a disagreement when I enter the house. "Petrus, how could you invite people over for dinner before checking with me?" Mum grumbles.

"I don't know, Nomse. I saw Mike and Susan in the department and I thought it would be a nice way to start making some friends," Dad says softly.

Mum shakes her head and sighs heavily. "But I'm on a deadline, Petrus. My editor wants the story by Monday."

I dart straight into my bedroom and shut the door. I lie on my bed, caressing my stuffed cat, Schrödinger. Dad gave it to me years ago when he told me all about Ervin Schrödinger, a brilliant Austrian physicist who did a lot of work in quantum mechanics. I stroke the cat's little white ears, heartsore and homesick for Cape Town. I think about my dear friends I left behind. Stacy, Black like me, was someone I could open my heart to. I could always count on her for support and comfort. My other best friend, Wendy, was White, but she was so different from Chrystal and Jennifer. She was completely in tune with me and would definitely not have made me feel uncomfortable about not using sunscreen. I miss them.

I turn on my computer, thinking about an e-mail message to send to Stacy. But the right words don't come to me. I glance at the diary lying on my desk, left there by my hopeful Mum. Better not say anything to her about how I'm feeling, or she'll make me write about it.

I get up, pace for a while, then with a sigh, flop down on the bed. Then I roll down onto the floor. My mind's driving me crazy. I've got to do something. Anything. I've got to figure out how to enjoy living in my new country. But where do I begin?

After a strangely quiet dinner in which Mum, Dad and I seem lost in our own thoughts, I return to my room and try to concentrate on my Algebra homework.

Dad knocks on my door and enters. "Thandi, hi sugar. Have you seen this article in the latest *New Scientist*?" Dad visits with me every evening before I go to sleep. It's our special time together when we chat about our day. It's also indoctrination time. Dad loves talking science with me and we often discuss current research and developments. He refuses to accept that science is a male domain. Unlike most kids I know who find their parents annoying and embarrassing, my Dad and I have a terrific relationship that I treasure.

"What is it, Dad?"

He wraps his flannel robe tighter around himself and flops down beside me. "There's this fifteen-year-old girl." He points to the article. "She's just invented a clever little toothbrush. A talking toothbrush! Here, look, it says '... Kirsten Levine has found the solution to getting boys and girls to brush regularly. Kids turn on their toothbrushes and listen to jokes while cleaning their teeth...'" Dad and I chuckle as we read more about the young inventor.

Dad runs his gentle fingers through my hair. "She reminds me of you, Thandi. Scientific and smart. When are you going to become famous?"

I smile at his handsome face and take off his thick-rimmed glasses. People always tell him he looks like Denzel Washington. He has a similar build too—tall and broad shouldered, only Dad has the beginnings of a belly. I don't look much like him, except for my mouth and chin, which are replicas of his. "Just you wait, Dad. Definitely before you're all grey." I clean his glasses with a tissue then put them back onto his face. He grins with his lips pinched together and gives me a hug. "Goodnight, sweetheart, I've got to be up early. Meeting with a graduate student at 8 a.m."

In the bathroom, as I squeeze out toothpaste onto my toothbrush, an idea pops into my mind. It's an amazing, thrilling idea that is sure to conquer my restlessness. Maybe it's the scientist in me itching to use my mind, or maybe it really is the answer to my problems.

What if I actually invented Thandi's TelePen,

the radio pen I wrote about for English? Back in my room, I pick up Shrodinger and look into his beady eyes. "Hey, why not? What about that toy bird I made for the science fair in sixth grade? I put a battery in it and when you pressed the buttons it would make different bird sounds. It won first place."

I flop on my bed and gaze at the wall. But what about my California babe image?

Whenever I need to clarify fuzzy thoughts, I have this weird habit of getting into a dialogue with myself. Gadgets are cool, I tell myself. Teens love them. Just think how they go on about iPods, MP3 players, fancy cell phones and stuff.

But can a gadget make it all okay?

Well, it's like an association thing, I rationalize. When you hear the name Pavlov, what do you think of? What about Freud? Not that I'll be anywhere in the same league as those guys. But the idea is the same. Instead of seeing my race, people will see my intellect.

I roll out of bed, walk back to the bathroom and stand in front of the bathroom mirror, beaming at my reflection. Then I get closer to the mirror and study my face. I study my flat Xhosa nose (thanks Mum) and thick Sotho lips, the lower one curling outward (thanks Dad). I close my eyes in an attempt to shut out the face that looks back at me in the mirror.

With a sigh, I turn off the bathroom light, return to my room and crawl under the covers. I can't change the way I look, but maybe I can change the way people look at me.

Chapter 5

"**Y**ou're up early for a Saturday morning." **Dad** looks up from his newspaper when I enter the kitchen, which smells of strong coffee.

"I have a lot to do today." I grab a slice of bread and stick it into the toaster. I've been wide awake since the first peep of light this morning. It's been just over a week since my decision to make the radio pen, and I've been obsessing about it every day. I've managed to convince myself I can do it, and now I can't wait to get started.

"Granny just phoned about half an hour ago," Dad says.

"Phoned? Does she know what a phone is?" I ask, finding it hard to picture my grandmother from "the other world" doing something as modern as talking on a phone.

Dad gives me a withering look.

"So, how is Granny?" I ask. "Poor thing. She looked so sad when we said good-bye to her."

"She's fine. She's worried about us." He gets

up and refills his coffee cup. "Mum would love it if we could get her over here to the States sometime."

Oh no! Granny here?

"But," Dad continues, unaware of the horror on my face, "I don't think there's any way we can convince her to get on an airplane. The idea of traveling out of the Cape is beyond her."

I breathe an inward sigh of relief.

"So what's all this work you have to do?" Dad asks, changing the subject.

"School stuff," I lie. "I have a long research assignment. So, I'll be in my room all day."

"You didn't have to do this much work at Siyafunda, and I paid good money to send you there." He takes a swig of coffee, then says, "Well, gee, Thandi, I was hoping you and I would spend the day together. Do a bit of exploring. Your mother is too busy. She wants to stay in and work."

I look at him in surprise. "*You* are not doing any research today? How come?" I reach for a glass and open the refrigerator.

Dad yawns and stretches. "I don't know. I guess I need a break. Been spending my days inside. I need to get out into the ocean for some samples. . ." His voice trails off. "By the way, what was that about a concert you were telling us yesterday?"

"Oh right, our school band will be performing on January 29. It's this big fundraising event at school. The flyer's right here on the refrigerator." I hastily pour myself a glass of orange juice.

Dad slides the flyer from under the refrigerator magnet, reads it and nods. "Good, I'll definitely be there. I heard great things about your principal. It'll give me an opportunity to meet her." He puts the flyer back on the refrigerator and starts picking up dirty dishes. "Anything I can do to help on your assignment?"

"No, but could you take me shopping later on?"

"What? Again?"

"What d'you mean, again, Dad? You've only taken me shopping once since we moved here—when I had to get clothes for school."

"Okay, you're right. What do you need?"

"Dad, I need a wet suit and a boogie board." A surfboard, too, but it's going to have to be one shock at a time. "Everyone here goes boogie boarding and surfing."

He frowns. "A boogie board? I thought they called it a surfboard." He dries his hands with a dish towel and looks at me sideways.

I toss my head in impatience. "Dad, when you go diving in the ocean, don't you see what the people around you are doing?" I fold my arms and shake my head at him. He drives Mum and me crazy because he is so oblivious. Mum says he has tunnel vision.

"So you're telling me they are different things?" His small eyes twinkle with amusement.

I nod. "Usually people first learn to boogie board before graduating to surfing, because it's easier."

"Aha, I see. Okay, I'll take you shopping later. I need to get a better dive suit for myself as well." He takes off his glasses and blows moist air onto them. "But this is it, Thandi. I'll get you a boogie board and a wet suit, but don't ask for a surfboard. Save your allowance for any of that fancy stuff. You know how I feel about spoiling kids."

I peck him on his smooth, clean-shaven cheek and dive back into my room. He's adorable even if he is a tightwad.

I'm so full of energy about tackling a new project I can hardly keep still. My plan is to sit at my desk and think long and hard how to go about the project, just like Dad and I did when I made the mechanical bird. I want to do this right, and I want to do it all by myself so it will be a total surprise to everyone when I'm finished. I settle into my chair and grab pencil and paper.

What do I want it to look like when it's all finished? There will be two objects that look like pens, but are broad enough to hold a small keypad and screen. One will transmit a message, and the other will receive it. Since both pens will be able to receive and relay messages, they have to be exactly the same.

I sit down at my computer and do online research on radio transmission. Hundreds of websites come up in a Google search. I click and read through the pages that come up. I'm caught in a fog of fascination, stopping only to bookmark websites and jot down book titles.

A knock on my door startles me so much that I let out a huge gasp. Mum comes in. "Thandi, are you okay?" The foolish grin on my face answers her question. She chuckles. "Darling, do you have any idea what the time is?"

I glance at the clock. "Oh my goodness! Is it really 1:00?" I've been working for four straight hours.

"Dad's waiting outside," she says. "Let's take a walk to the café down on the beach and get something to eat."

Outside, I notice for the first time just how beautiful the winding trail is that connects our house to the beach. I have the impulse to run up close to every tree and shrub we pass and examine and sniff them, like a puppy on its evening stroll.

Seagulls flutter and squawk above us. A hummingbird with a ruby neck and a light green body hovers about a yard from me, and then with a sudden swoop it lands on a pretty red flower. The air smells of licorice, mingled with ocean saltiness. The sky is clear and a light breeze fans the grass and trees. When the ocean comes in full view, I sprint ahead, stopping only when I get right to the water's edge.

I gaze at the massive Pacific. It looks so proud and powerful, two qualities I covet. I inhale deeply, comforted by my decision to make the radio pen. It's the perfect prescription. I just know it.

Mum, Dad, and I head to the café and get seated at a table on the terrace. The aroma of seafood awakens my hunger. As we study the menu, I hear lively chatter from somewhere behind us. I turn around. At the corner table I see three smiling Black girls midway through a lunch of hamburgers. One of them is Ciara from Buena Vista High. She notices me and waves. On impulse I go up to their table.

"Hey, Thandi," she greets me. "Meet my friends. This is Tasha, our principal's daughter, and this is Juliet." My jaw drops. Tasha has café au lait skin and frizzy, brown hair. I would never have guessed that the blue-eyed Ms. Moore had a Black daughter. The three girls burst into laughter at my expression. I smile, embarrassed.

"Hi," I say, wearing my friendliest smile. I want in here. Supportive "sistas" may be what I need to cure my unhappiness.

"Thandi is from South Africa," Ciara informs them.

Tasha's eyebrows lift and she reaches for my elbow. "Mom told us about you. Wanna sit with us?" I want you to tell us about South Africa." Her warmth and California-style Southern drawl make me feel right at home with them.

"I'll go tell my folks and get some money. Be right back."

"She'll be right back," I hear Ciara say, mocking my accent.

When I join them again, they have a chair ready for me between Tasha and Ciara. I try to catch Juliet's eye. But dark sunglasses make that impossible. Besides, her attention is on her iPod. She's wearing headphones and scrolling through her iPod menu. Unlike the other two, she takes no interest in me. Or pretends not to, anyway.

"What grade are you guys in?" I ask.

"We're all sophomores," Tasha says, "but we go to different schools."

"I go to Dos Pueblos High," Juliet says, looking up suddenly. She takes off one earphone. I turn puzzled eyes to her. Her sunglasses are disconcerting. I can't tell if she's looking at me or not. Her broad face is covered in acne. Large gold hoops hang from her ears.

"We live in Sycamore Canyon," Tasha says. "Different school district."

"Rich folks' district," Juliet says. "White schools." She looks in my direction. "I live on the West side? In those apartments where all the Latinos live?" She expresses her statements like questions.

"White kids don't come to our school," she adds. "They too scared of the gangs?"

The waiter, a red-faced guy, comes to take my order. I point to the board with the specials. "I'll have the special salad—organic greens and grilled goat cheese."

The three girls exchange grins. "What?" I ask.

"That's White folks' food," Ciara says. "*Rich* White folks. Organic greens? Grilled goat cheese?"

"Oh. What should I have ordered?"

"What should I have ordered?" Juliet says, mocking my accent.

"Real food," says Ciara. "Hamburgers, fried chicken, the good stuff. Know what I'm saying?"

I shrug my shoulders and lean back, not sure if

she's just kidding around.

Mum is so into healthy food and so against fast food that I never consider those options when we eat out. We tend to be adventurous with food, ordering things that are new and interesting to us. Plus, in health-conscious California, I figured most people eat like we do. When I see Juliet's smirk, I signal to the waiter and order a regular hamburger.

"And a side of french fries," Ciara shouts to him. She holds up her hand to me for a high five.

"How did you guys get to be friends if you don't go to the same school?" I ask.

"We go way back," Tasha says. "Our families all go to Grace Baptist Church on Lower State Street. We met up there when we were this small." She holds up her hand about three feet from the floor.

"So when did you come to Buena Vista?" asks Tasha.

"A few days after Christmas. We've only been here three weeks now."

"Fresh off the boat," Ciara says. "Can tell from the natural." She points to my head with her eyes.

Ciara's insult is like a splash of cold water on my face. I feel myself getting worked up the same way I do when I try to persuade Mum that I need to have my hair relaxed.

"Maybe natural is *in* in Africa," Juliet says. They all giggle.

Natural is anything but *in* among teens in South Africa. I take deep breaths to make my voice come out as close to normal as possible. "It's because of my Mum," I say defensively and point to Mum, who's sitting a few tables away from us. Her cropped kinky hair is a source of pride. "She always talks about how in the '80's when they were students in South Africa they risked their lives in the fight for freedom. And now that we are free she's not about to give it up by messing with her hair. That's how she sees it. If she straightened her hair, she would be giving up her freedom to be a Black woman."

"That's heavy stuff, girl," Ciara says, her eyes on Mum. "Natural suits your mom, though. Gives her that professional look. She sure is skinny. Eating them organic greens."

The waiter brings me my hamburger. I grin at Mum's horrified expression. Ciara passes me a sauce bottle. "Spice it up, girl." I squeeze some brown sauce onto the burger and take a huge bite.

"Good?" Tasha asks.

I nod, even though it tastes like hot cardboard to me.

"I guess it's different in Africa where all the sistas have kinky hair," Ciara says, picking up our earlier thread. "Around here, those of us who don't have 'good' hair,"—she pauses to give the word "good" air quotes—"relax it and pretend we were born that way." There's a quality of drama to her speech that comes from her stressing every other word.

Juliet's scowl—her default expression—morphs into a smile. Tasha laughs in agreement. I look at her gold-tinged ringlets, which I assume are natural.

Then, I turn to Juliet's braids which are bunched up at the crown. Definitely extensions. In fact, I can even see the difference in the color between her hair and the braids. I look at Ciara, who has straight, shoulder-length hair. "Yes, I relax my hair," she says to me. "I don't buy that 'freedom' b.s. You think Oprah does?"

Boy or girl? Male or female? I pour ketchup over my fries and stuff my mouth so I won't have to say anything. Sooner or later, I'm going to have to address my hair. Not now, though, while I have other things to digest.

Juliet rocks her shoulders to her music. "Who you listening to?" Tasha asks. Juliet sticks an earphone into Tasha's ear.

"Honey Ain't Sweet. You like them?" Her face is turned to me so I brace myself to answer.

"I don't know their music."

Silence. A silence that shouts. I shrink back and reach for my glass of water. Then, to make up for this apparent faux pas, I say, "The Spades is the group I love." I lean back, awaiting my kudos.

In my frantic attempts to be up on popular culture, I memorized the lyrics to this West Coast rap group's most popular songs. I found out from *Today's Teen* that The Spades, a trio of Black guys who grew up in the Oakland projects, is the hottest rap group on the youth music scene in America.

To my astonishment the girls exchange the same mocking looks as when I ordered the salad of organic greens. I look into my plate and keep taking sips of water.

"The Spades is White kids' music," Ciara spits out a couple beats later.

I bite my lip and sink lower into my seat.

"Sell outs, them dudes. Lyrics for White kids who don't know shit about what it's like to be Black." Juliet's voice drips with disgust.

Talk about a double faux pas! I want to disappear, but at the same time I feel ready to explode. I yank my chair back and spring up. "So you guys think I'm not Black enough. I eat White folks' food. I listen to White kids' music. You know what? I don't have to take this petty crap." I slam the $20 bill I got from Dad on the table and stomp off.

This encounter takes me back to South Africa and the issues Black kids had among themselves. Different factors played into those conflicts though. In South Africa, Blacks seemed to fall into one of three groups: tribal, township people, and middle class.

Tribal people, folks in *the other world,* still live untouched by the Industrial Revolution. Women paint their faces with red mud and balance buckets of water on their heads to carry them from streams to their homes. Men ride around in donkey carts, and half-naked kids roam among the cattle in open fields. Mum and Dad grew up in such an environment, but they were sent to privately-funded schools which led them into the city.

The township people, most of whom are very poor, live in crowded areas on the outskirts of the cities. Back during the days of apartheid, Blacks were needed to work as laborers in the cities, so the White government created these townships since Whites didn't want to live near Blacks.

With apartheid gone, Black people now have more opportunities, resulting in a growing Black middle class. And that's the category to which I belonged. We middle class Black kids turned our noses up at the township and tribal kids. They were beneath us. Township kids hated us back, accusing us of being 'White.' But they also looked down upon the tribal kids.

The kids from the tribal areas didn't hate anyone. They envied us city kids, dreaming of the day when they too could join the mainstream of modern South Africa.

I gaze at the calm ocean when I return to Mum and Dad, who are stooped over the check. A sailboat glides serenely toward the nearby islands. I try to turn my thoughts to my radio pen to force myself out of the foul mood that threatens to swallow me.

"Ready for some shopping?" Dad asks, putting on his coat. And the prospect of owning a boogie board and a wet suit, and all that they promise, does the job for me.

Chapter
6

"Ladies and gentleman, welcome to Buena Vista High's Annual Concert," Ms. Moore announces to the audience of students and parents assembled in the school auditorium. "I hand you over to our music director, Mr. Bennett, who will start the program with our choir singing the school anthem."

My eyes follow Ms. Moore to her seat. Mum and Dad mentioned they wanted to talk to her during the break. When Ms. Moore sits down, I notice Tasha on one side of her and a guy who has to be Tasha's brother, on the other side. My gaze fixes on his thick, shoulder-length dreadlocks. His face is buried in a magazine. There's something about his appearance that intrigues me. I can't wait to talk to him. I turn my glance back to Tasha. Her lovely hair ripples over her shoulders. I hope she's not mad at me after the café incident. I'll apologize to her and explain that it's all because I'm new here. I'm just learning how to fit in.

After what seems like an eternity, the announcement from Mr. Bennett finally comes. "Ladies and gentleman, we will take a twenty minute break, and when we return our sophomore brass band will commence the second half of the program with Rossini's 'William Tell Overture'."

I nudge Mum, and we cross over to Ms. Moore. Tasha, to my relief, gives me a wide grin. She has deep dimples, which I hadn't noticed the other day.

"Salif, this is Thandi. Remember I told you I met her at Paradise Beach Café?"

"*Jambo*," he says, standing up. His long-sleeved T-shirt is tucked into jeans that sit comfortably on his hips. No chance of them falling even a fraction. He looks straight into my eyes.

"What's *jambo*?" I ask.

Salif jerks his head back in surprise. "You don't know? It's Swahili for hello." Like his sister, he has a narrow nose with tiny nostrils.

"Oh, I don't know Swahili," I respond.

"You don't? I thought all Africans knew some Swahili," Tasha says and knits her brows. I knit my brows too. The warm, sing-songy drawl I heard at the café, is gone. Tasha's voice is now completely neutral.

"You know, I never got around to asking you about South Africa at the café," Tasha continues. "By the way, you were awesome that day. Ciara deserved that. She's going through her 'I'm totally Black, OK?' phase."

"Pot calling the kettle black," Salif says,

grinning.

"What do you mean by that?" Tasha glares at him.

I smile at the floor, knowing exactly what he's referring to.

"So what's your language?" Tasha asks me.

"My language?" I ask, furrowing my forehead. "English."

"She means the language of your tribe," Salif says. "What tribe do you belong to?" His accusing tone and challenging demeanor make me tense up.

The question leaves me speechless. The word "tribe" jars on my nerves. It evokes images of half-naked people with animal skins wrapped around their bodies.

"I - uh - I don't know." Not entirely a lie considering that Mum is Xhosa and Dad is Sotho. And since neither speaks the other's language, English has been the only language spoken in our home.

Salif peers into my eyes. I feel like he can see right into me and read my thoughts. It's unsettling. His handsome face displays an intensity and a hint of arrogance. This is a smart guy. A thinker. I can tell. A part of me is drawn to him, but another part of me wants to get away from him. Suddenly I find myself longing to be with Jennifer and Chrystal. It's so much easier with them.

I scan the audience. I notice Chrystal's little sister Chloe, then Linda, her stepmom. Finally, I see Chrystal. "I have to go," I say to Salif and Tasha, and flee.

"Hey, Chrystal, how come you weren't on stage?" I ask. She's in the freshman brass band. Chloe runs into my arms when she sees me and starts chattering away. But when I notice the expression on Chrystal's face, my heart skips a beat. She stares at the floor looking like she's about to burst into tears. More than anything I want her to look up and with that mischievous grin of hers, say, "Hi, Thandi To-mah-to."

"Chrystal, what's wrong?" She doesn't stir or shift her gaze. I look at Linda, hoping she'll explain the problem.

Linda shrugs and says, "I think she wants to be left alone right now." I nod, wave goodbye to Chloe and leave.

As we drive home from the concert, Mum and Dad gush about their conversation with Ms. Moore.

"She's invited us to her house for dinner in a couple weeks," Mum says. "And we'll have them over at our place after that. Oh, and she's asked Dad to come to your school as a guest presenter."

"That's right, Thandi," Dad says. "She asked if I would do a presentation on marine biology for the freshman class."

"Are you going to do it, Dad?" I ask, thrilled. I'm really proud of my dad's achievements as a marine biologist, and it will be great to have my class see how smart he is.

"Oh, sure," Dad says. "We'll have to sit down together and decide what my talk should be about."

"Ms. Moore was married to a man from Kenya," Mum says. "So her children are half Kenyan. And she says they are crazy about everything that has to do with Africa."

"Isn't that wonderful, Thandi?" Dad says. "Perfect friends for you."

I get quiet, reflecting on how mixed up I felt when Salif was around. I wonder if it was that hint of arrogance that made me want to get away from him.

As we turn onto our tree-lined road, with its row of elegant houses in our middle-class neighborhood, I think about Saturday's conversation with the sistas at Paradise Café. It brings me to a question I have to figure out. What does it mean to be Black in America?

Chapter 7

I'm on my way from Algebra class to my locker when I notice the flyer on the big bulletin board in the hallway.

Talent Show—March 14
Do you have a unique talent that demonstrates originality and imagination? Show it off at the annual talent show. Top three contestants win $100 each. *Enroll at the Drama Department.*

One hundred dollars would help a lot toward a used surfboard. I read the flyer again. I do have a talent, one I want badly to showcase to the world. I glance at my watch to see if I have enough time to enroll before the next period. March 13 is about six weeks from now. It should give me enough time to finish up my radio pen, my ticket out of everything that seems wrong in my life. I couldn't have asked for a better opportunity to show off my invention and get some money too. That is if I win.

"Hi there."

"Jennifer! Where were you last night?"

"We couldn't make it to the concert. Dad worked late. Want some?" She holds out a small bag of cashews.

"Sure." Not enough time to make it to the drama department right now.

We wander toward a bench in the sun. The ground is squelchy from last night's rain. A chilly breeze has me shivering.

Jennifer zips up her fleece vest and pushes her hands into her pockets. "Wish the weather would improve. You haven't had a chance to try out your boogie board and wet suit yet."

I shrug. "No biggie. I think they're forecasting nice weather for the weekend."

Jennifer sighs. "Wonder when Chrystal's going to get out of her funk."

"What's up with her?" I ask.

"I don't know. I wish she'd tell me what's wrong. All I know is that she can't see her mom this Sunday. She usually spends Sundays with her."

"Only Sundays? How come?"

"Some arrangement her parents made when they got divorced. Her mom lives in LA. She's this bigwig photographer. She drives up here on Sundays to be with Chrystal."

"I can't even begin to imagine seeing my mum only once a week," I muse.

"Well, there is a plus side. Vacation time.

Chrystal spends every single vacation with her mom, and once a year they go to neat places like Tahiti and Paris and stuff. Chrystal's been all over the world."

"Except Africa," I say.

Jennifer gives a dismissive shrug. "Africa isn't exactly number one on people's list of places to visit."

The comment stings. I rehearse a line about Cape Town's beauty, but I decide against getting defensive.

After a pause, Jennifer says, "Let's do something fun on Sunday. Take Chrystal's mind off whatever it is."

I nod. "Great idea. But what can we do that she'll really like? Boogie boarding?"

Jennifer's lips curve into a smile. "I know something she'll enjoy even more. She loves riding her bike on the coast path to the bird sanctuary. Let's go bike riding on Sunday."

"Okay," comes my automatic reply. "What time?" I must be losing my mind. Not only do I not have a bicycle, I've never ridden a bike in my life. Cape Town's steep, narrow roads robbed me of this pleasure.

The bell rings and we traipse to our lockers, get out our World History books, and head for class.

Inside, Mr. Roth is frowning. "How long does it take you guys to settle down?" Neurotic about punctuality, he always starts class right on the dot. Students fear this loud, strict teacher as if he were Zeus himself. We scramble to our seats and get our books out.

"Class," Mr. Roth begins in his boring monotone, "as you all know, the United States is a nation of immigrants. Except for the Native Americans, the only indigenous people of the country, everyone has come here from some other part of the world." He pauses and looks at each of us in turn.

The classroom feels stuffy and overheated. I yawn and stretch my eyes open to keep from nodding off. A fire engine's siren blares past the school. Mr. Roth glances out the window then draws a long breath. With a distant look in his eyes, he says, "My ancestors came from Ireland, France, and England." He pulls down the world map and points. "Here is Ireland, and next to it, England, and here's France."

I stare at his graying beard wondering where this is all leading.

"Your next assignment …"

The whole class lets out a groan.

"… is to research your ancestry."

I sit up, my ears on sudden super alert.

"For this assignment you will be researching who your ancestors are, where they came from, their culture and so on. You have five weeks for this assignment, and then you'll be required to do a presentation in front of the class."

I crack my knuckles. Can I pretend I didn't hear any of this?

Mr. Roth walks to the back of the room, unrolls a map of the world and pins it on the back wall. "Here's a world map for this class. I have a map for each of my five classes, so be sure you watch where I'm pinning yours. The first thing I'd like you to do is to make little flags of the country or countries your ancestors came from. Then, glue the flag to a toothpick and stick it into the map right on the country, like this." He stabs a little flag on a toothpick into Ireland on the world map. "And finally, on the last day of our presentations we will have a feast. I'm going to send out letters to your parents informing them of this assignment and asking if they'll be able to contribute a dish from your ancestors' countries."

My heart sinks. The last thing in the world I need is to draw attention to something that will give people more reasons to tease, stare, or ask dumb questions.

I sigh. When will I have time to do this assignment anyway? I mean I have higher priorities, like inventing Thandi's TelePen.

And with a start, I realize I've got something even more urgent to do. I've got to figure out how to get Dad to buy me a bicycle. Then I've got to learn how to ride it before Sunday.

Chapter
8

Dad's car pulls into the driveway. I rehearse my line one more time. *Dad, I know you don't believe in spoiling kids. I wouldn't be asking for a bicycle if I thought it was something frivolous. I honestly need a bicycle because. . .*

"Hi Sugar, are you okay?" Dad grins as he approaches the house.

I peck him on his cheek. "Yeah, fine. Dad, have you ever had a bicycle?"

He squints at me, then heads straight for the kitchen. I follow him. He empties a glass of water into his mouth. "Funny that you ask about a bicycle, Thandi. As I was driving home today I was actually thinking about getting bikes for us."

"Really?"

"I drove past a used bicycle store. I couldn't believe how inexpensive they are."

Mum joins us in the kitchen. "Bicycles? I want

one too, Petrus. Have you noticed how well this town is set up for biking?"

Looks like I'm going to have no problem acquiring a bike.

"Yah, I noticed lovely bike paths along the coast and to the university too," Dad responds.

Mum waves a hand across his slightly bulging tummy. "You should bike to campus, you know. It'll be great exercise."

He nods. "Not a bad idea." He turns to the pile of mail on the counter and shuffles through the envelopes.

Time for me to make my next move. "Dad, I was wondering, um, would it be possible to get the bikes, like, today?" That would leave me tomorrow and Saturday to learn how to ride.

"*Like* today?" Dad exclaims, looking up. "Thandi, you're beginning to sound like a Californian."

I smile, grabbing Dad's comment and clutching it close to me.

Mum stretches. "I could use a little break before starting dinner prep. Why don't we go check out the bikes at that store before it closes?"

Dad gets out his keys. "Sure." We drive to the used bicycle store close to the university. It isn't long before I see something I like. The bike frame is black with soft, easy-to-grip handles. And at $60, it's a steal.

I fall in love with it at once, suddenly realizing the independence a bike will give me. I picture

Jennifer, Chrystal, and myself cruising down the bike path along the beach. Another step toward my California babe transformation.

◊◊◊◊◊

I wake up bright and early on Saturday morning to the crooning of Hugh Masekela, one of Dad's favorite South African jazz artists. The sweet aroma of pancakes wafts through the house. Dad must be in the kitchen preparing his special blueberry pancake breakfast. After a shower I pull on my grey sweatpants and a lime green sweater. I love bright colors. I flinch at my reflection in the mirror as I reach for my comb. After Ciara's 'fresh off the boat' comment I can never look at my hair without getting intensely worked up. Maybe I should get a wig. I groan and join Dad in the kitchen.

"Morning, morning, Sugar," he sings, blowing me a kiss, and tossing a pancake at the same time. "Let's have a good, hearty breakfast, then give you your next round of bike riding lessons. Oh, you're going to love it. *Eh-heh.*"

Yesterday, when Dad got home from work, he gave me my first bike riding lessons, and I was a miserable failure. I was so clumsy and so nervous about falling off that I seemed to make no progress at all. And now, nervousness about whether today will be an improvement snuffs out my appetite for what is usually my favorite breakfast. "Dad, how about one tiny lesson before we eat?"

"Oh, okay, let me get a few pancakes ready for Mum, first. Why don't you go get your bicycle out of the garage?"

Dad joins me a few minutes later and eases me onto the seat of my bicycle. He shows me again how to rest my hands on the bars and helps me keep my balance as I pump the pedals. I can feel my confidence building and I'm able to relax and enjoy the feeling of being on a bike.

"Okay, time for breakfast, then you can practice more." Dad stops the bike and shows me how to climb down. "It's a funny thing with learning how to ride. Some people learn it in no time, and others, well . . ." and he shrugs.

With a gulp, I cross as many fingers as I can. I better be the type to learn in no time.

I gobble down a pancake, chug my orange juice, and dash back outside. I lean the bike toward me, climb onto the seat, put my right foot on the pedal, and start moving. The other foot is in the air ready to touch the ground if I feel I'm about to fall.

Dad walks toward me. "That's great." He holds one of the handles and encourages me to get both my feet on the pedals. After a little while I'm confident enough to wheel myself around, right foot on the pedal, left foot in the air, ready to touch the ground if I lose my balance.

"You don't need me anymore," Dad observes. "Actually, let me lower the seat a little more so that you can put your feet on the ground easily."

My ears latch on to Dad's accent: his

pronunciation, *"uhctually,"* *"thuht"* and a Sotho rhythm in the way he speaks. It's something I hadn't paid any attention to before.

I get back on the bicycle with just my right foot on the pedal and let it roll down the road. I love the feeling of the ride and the cool foggy air blowing lightly on my face. I feel a sense of freedom. A sense that nothing matters. Not my color or my ancestors or any teasing. Just the pleasure of being on this wonderful pair of wheels.

But, I'm not really riding my bike yet. Even after an hour I find that every time I try to move my left foot toward the pedal I lose my balance. Why on earth can't I get past this stage?

And why did I get myself into this mess?

I take a serious look at the bicycle. I can get the bike moving with both my feet off the ground. It shouldn't be any problem to have both my feet on the pedals. But as soon as I do that, the bike veers sharply to the right, and I crash to the ground. Shaken and a little bruised, I look up, hoping nobody witnessed my incompetence. I spot a blue vest and realize in horror that Mr. Britannica is coming toward me. I lift myself up as quickly as I can, grab the bike, and hobble to my house.

That was close. What is Peter doing here? And why won't he leave me alone?

◊◊◊◊◊

"Hi, Jennifer? It's Thandi. Hey, I can't make

it today."

"Why?" Jennifer asks.

"I . . . I . . . My parents . . . We're going out for the day."

"O-kay." Jennifer sounds disappointed.

"Jennifer, I . . . I'm sorry. I really wanted to be with you and Chrystal today, but . . . I can't."

"Liar!" I hiss to myself as I put the phone down. Gloom wraps itself around me. I flop down on the living room couch, close to tears. More than anything I want to be out having fun with my friends right now.

I curse Dad for being anti-TV. I desperately need something mindless to distract me. No, I don't. I need to work on my radio pen. I pull myself up with a sudden burst of energy and head to my room.

Stretched out on my bed, I examine the three books about radio-operated gadgets that I checked out from the library. A book with clear pictures gives me ideas that excite me. I need to program a computer microchip for the Telepen. A lot of what I read is very difficult to understand.

After a couple of hours of intense reading, I close my books and lie on my bed, staring at the white ceiling. From the living room comes the muffled nasal voice of a National Public Radio announcer. My brain feels like it's about to explode with all the information I've packed into it. This whole project feels pretty overwhelming right now. I wish I had someone to talk to about it.

To relax my mind, I page through the latest

Today's Teen magazine. In the back are ads of teenagers in body suits holding longboards with colorful ocean designs. I lapse into a dream in which I'm dressed in my wet suit, riding the waves like it's second nature. The cool sea air fans my face and my lips taste of salt. Acquiring a surfboard has become an obsession with me, especially because Jennifer and Chrystal go on and on and on about surfing. I return to the magazine and look at the prices of the surfboards. $300! Yikes! It's going to have to be a used one, unless I can persuade Dad to help out with the balance after I win the contest. If I win. If I can actually make the device . . .

Mum comes into my room. "Hey, darling, want to practice riding your bike?" An oversized denim shirt makes her petiteness more pronounced.

I jump up with a smile and stretch. "Good idea, Mum. I think it's just what I need." We get our bikes out of the garage and wheel them out to the road. Mum helps me keep my balance as I ride with both legs on the pedals.

"Okay, it's time for you to try it on your own, now," she says. "Just keep practicing. You'll get there. I'm going to ride around the block."

I roll down the sidewalk with one foot on the pedal and the other foot dangling in the air when I hear a voice. "A-hem, hello Thandi."

I freeze on my bike, lose my balance, put my left foot on the ground to prevent a fall, and whirl my head around. It's Mr. Britannica. He's dressed in a crisp white shirt and black trousers, and it isn't even a school day. What a weirdo.

Peter looks at me, a timid smile on his face. I know I can't escape. And I don't have the energy to be rude to him. My main concern is how much has he seen, and how much did he see yesterday? I meet his eyes and mumble, "Hi."

"Learning to ride a bike?"

His gentle voice surprises me. My face gets hot. I nod.

He frowns at my bike then looks up. "I've got this new bike with these really nice wide tires. I bet it will be easier for you to learn how to balance on that one."

Before I can open my mouth, he turns and runs up the road. I wonder if I should flee to my house, but I'm too bewildered to act. In a couple minutes, Peter's back on a bicycle. A spiffy bicycle with a shiny blue frame and wide tires with deep tread.

My cheap, used bicycle looks so shabby and old-fashioned compared to his. And it suddenly occurs to me that Chrystal and Jennifer probably have fancy bicycles too, and would probably have been horrified when they saw mine. But with the many things I've been asking for, it would take real talent to get Dad to indulge me in an expensive bike too.

"Try this, Thandi," Peter says. "My father got me this bike for Christmas. It's amazingly easy to ride." He holds the bike out to me.

I slowly get off my bike, too dazed to do anything else. With a racing heart, I get on his bike. This whole learning-to-ride-a-bike thing is way more stressful than I expected. I do my usual thing of one foot on the pedal, the other in the air, and glide down the sidewalk. Peter rides alongside me on my bicycle. "All you need, Thandi, is self-confidence. Just do it. Put both your feet on the pedals."

I can't. What if I fall?

"Take the plunge, Thandi. I promise, you'll be fine," comes Peter's encouraging voice.

Slowly, I pluck up the courage and place my dangling foot on the other pedal. To my surprise, the bike remains steady as it smoothly rolls along. I pedal slowly, tentatively, then gradually faster. The road inclines and I have to pedal harder. And, with a rush of joy, I realize that I am actually riding a bicycle.

I love the cool breeze on my face. I'm going downhill now. No need to pedal. Time to turn around and return to Peter. "Peter, how can I ever thank you? It was, it was, oh, I loved it," and I'm giggling, delirious with joy at my accomplishment.

He shrugs. "Oh, you're more than welcome. Isn't it funny how with most skills it's just a matter of self-confidence? I think if you ride my bike a little more you'll build up enough confidence to ride your own."

Peter speaks in a most unusual manner: slowly, clearly, and like an adult. In class he only speaks when the teacher asks him a question, and he almost always answers in a single word. Now, as I hear him speak in full sentences, it's as if he has rehearsed everything he says. He has a soft, and very appealing voice. The kind of voice you can listen to forever.

"So where do you live?" I ask.

"Over there. See that white house with the black, sloping roof?" He points to a cute A-frame house up a block from where we are. "What about you?"

"Oh, this is my house right here in front of us."

He nods. "I like the Spanish style."

"Is that a Spanish style?"

"Well, you know, the red-tiled roof and arches and things. A lot of buildings around here are like that."

"I guess I haven't paid much attention."

Guilt about the way I ignored him presses on me. How do you say you're sorry when you've been unfriendly to someone for weeks? On an impulse I ask, "Shall we ride some more, maybe a little past this block?" And then, as soon as the words are out, I regret the suggestion. What would Chrystal and Jennifer say if they saw me with Peter?

"Sure." His face relaxes into a bashful smile.

Mum appears at that moment. I completely forgot about her. She rides up to us, and grinning at me on Peter's bike, she says, "Wow, where did that snazzy thing come from?"

"It's mine," Peter responds. "Thandi's been riding it like a pro."

"Mum, this is Peter. He's a freshman at my school too. Want to see me ride?" I do a wide circle around the road.

"Wonderful!" Mum exclaims. She beams at Peter. "Thank you, Peter. I just didn't know how to get her to do the final step. Oh, that's great." Then she turns to me. "Thandi, I need to get back and start dinner. Don't be out too long, okay?"

Peter and I ride up a few blocks in our neighborhood. He shows me how to change gears up a hill and how to brake gently for a downward slope. After about a half an hour of riding, my legs start aching and I'm panting like crazy. I get off the bike and rest on the sidewalk. Peter stops in front of me. "You're doing remarkably well."

"Thanks." I watch him as he sits at the edge of the seat and begins tapping his toes and looking around. I want to ask why he stares at me and keeps trying to talk to me, but I don't know how to phrase it in a polite way. An old man and his shaggy-haired dog walk past us.

"Peter, how come you, you know, uh, stare so much?" I take a deep breath and hug my legs.

He rests his eyes on my face, the timid smile returns, and says, "I'm sorry. I guess I've never seen anyone as attractive as you before."

I gulp. Me attractive? Is he being sarcastic?

"I should go," he says. "Maybe we'll do this again. Tomorrow?" He gives me a hopeful look.

No, it can't be sarcasm. Look how nice he's been to me. "Sure," I blurt out, knowing full well this is the wrong answer. If anybody at school finds out, I'll be toast. Jennifer and Chrystal will drop me instantly. And I can't afford to lose their friendship.

He takes his bike from me, waves good-bye, and rides away. I crack my knuckles and stare at his back. I should go after him and tell him I'm not available tomorrow. But, I don't have the courage to do that.

Mum calls from the porch. "Thandi, dinner is in five minutes."

As I walk my bike to the garage, Peter's words echo in my mind. *I guess I've never seen anyone as attractive as you before.* I smile.

Then I bite my lower lip. What am I going to do about that 'date' tomorrow?

Chapter 9

During English class I try to make eye contact with Jennifer and Chrystal, but the ever-alert Mrs. Stevens looks right at me as soon as she senses any body movement. First period seems to go on forever. I'm dying to find out about their day of cycling and whether Chrystal is okay. Boy, I sure could have used my radio pen today.

When the bell finally rings, I trot over to Chrystal. We head down the hall for second period. She has a wide grin on her face. "Thandi To-mah-to, guess what!" I smile, relieved to see her so chirpy. Yesterday's bike ride must have worked.

Jennifer joins us as we shuffle down the hallway. "Do we have an idea, or what!" They are both full of giggles.

"What is it?"

"We have a great idea for the talent show," Chrystal bursts out. "We'll tell you all about it later." Grinning at me mysteriously, they both break into the chorus to 'Sun and Moon,' the title song on The Spades' current album.

I frown at them, then anxious to impress, I join in the singing. "You're going to love our idea," Jennifer says as we head for our seats.

I narrow my eyes at her. After the boogie board and bicycle ideas, I can't help wondering what new weakness of mine is about to be exposed.

After fourth period, Jennifer and Chrystal pull me to a quiet corner away from the other students. "We're thinking of starting a band," Chrystal says.

Jennifer mimes playing a guitar and sings a verse from 'Sun and Moon.' "See I've been learning to play the guitar for a few months now, okay, and Chrystal plays the sax, right."

"All we need is a drummer. Can you try the drums, Thandi?" Chrystal's eyes are wide with excitement.

I step back, frowning at them. "I'm not the least bit musical, guys."

"But, but you'll love it," Jennifer gushes. "I mean think how cool it will be to have our own band. We can start out singing The Spades' songs and then we can start composing and producing our own stuff. Is that cool or what?"

Can't deny it. My radio pen invention seems pretty nerdy in comparison. I look at Chrystal's elated face and wish I could let out a big, "Yes, yes, let's do it." I want to be caught up in their excitement. But when I picture myself banging on drums, I have to say it feels so hypocritical. It just isn't me. Besides, nerdy or not, people are going to love using the radio pen. I can't pass up this perfect opportunity to show it off and have a new identity bestowed on me. Then there's the money to consider. If Chrystal, Jennifer, and I win, which I doubt given what amateurs we are, the money would have to be split three ways. Not an appealing idea.

I look down at the grass and shake my head. "I'm sorry. I already have plans for the talent show."

They jerk their heads toward me. "What? You already have plans?" Jennifer explodes. "So, what . . . what're you going to do?"

I sigh. "I can't tell you."

Chrystal flashes accusing eyes at me. "Thandi, I thought we were friends."

"Yeah," Jennifer adds, "friends don't have secrets."

Ouch! My secrets from them are mounting.

"Listen, you guys are my very best friends here in Buena Vista. This thing for the talent show, well, it's something I can't really explain. It's a . . . a surprise!"

They snort and turn to walk away. Jennifer nudges Chrystal. "Must be some weird African thing," she says, and they both snicker.

I flinch. We avoid each other the rest of the day.

As soon as I get home, I take out my bike and head for Peter's house. I know I shouldn't be doing this. Especially with the way things are between Chrystal, Jennifer, and me. But I can't seem to help myself. I mean, I'm not a flake, and I did agree to getting together with Peter.

I walk my bike past pretty stucco homes that have bright bougainvillea flowers draping their banks. With its Swiss cottage shape, Peter's house is the most unusual on our street. I put my finger on the doorbell and pause. It's not too late to turn around. Suddenly the door opens and Peter is in front of me, smiling. "I saw you coming from my window," he says.

Sometimes decisions get made for you! "Ready?" I ask.

He nods. "Uh-huh, but I can't be out for long. My dad needs my help on something." He looks at my bicycle. "Did you ride it yet?"

"No, I still don't feel ready."

"Well, maybe after today you'll be more sure of yourself." He rolls his bicycle out onto the road and hands it to me. "Want to ride down to the beach?"

He climbs on my bike and we roll down the hill. "So, how come you're in Buena Vista?" he asks.

"My dad was hired as a professor at the university."

"Oh, right, your dad's a scientist, a marine biologist, right?"

"Uh-huh. One of the top in his field, in fact." Bragging about my dad comes too easily to me.

"He's coming to our school one of these days, right?"

"Yes. Ms. Moore invited him to do a presentation because, well, I guess marine biology is a big part of what we're doing this year in biology."

"I'm looking forward to your dad's talk. I find ocean life fascinating," Peter remarks. "My dad's a scientist too."

"Oh really? What kind of scientist is he?"

"A physicist. He's doing research in superstring theory at U.C.B.V." He smiles at my confused look. "University of California at Buena Vista."

I smile sheepishly because I should have known that. "What a coincidence that our dads work at the same place."

"So how does your dad do research? Does he have specimens in an aquarium in his lab or something?"

I shake my head. "Oh no. He studies specimens in their natural environments. There's this family of fish he specializes in and he goes diving in the ocean to study them."

"Are these fish in the Atlantic or Pacific?"

"Both. Different species in the Pacific but belonging to the same family of fish he worked with while we were in Cape Town."

Peter throws me a look of admiration. "That sounds really exciting. Have you ever gone diving with him?"

"No, I've never been interested. Besides it seems a very adult undertaking."

We turn into a busier road. I feel myself tensing up as cars whiz past me. Then we turn into a narrow, quieter road that goes uphill. Peter gets further and further ahead of me. Suddenly I can't see him. I cycle up and down and turn the corner and back. He isn't anywhere.

"Thandi! Thandi, over here, by the eucalyptus." I turn to the direction of his voice. His bicycle, mine that is, is leaning against a giant tree. I suddenly see him just beyond the tree, beckoning. In a low voice he says, "This is the butterfly grove. Come, I'll show you the monarch butterflies."

We creep through the grass and shrubs and come to a little clearing surrounded by tall eucalyptus trees. Hundreds, no thousands, of orange and black butterflies flutter about, and thousands more plaster the branches of the trees. What an incredible sight!

We are only a few yards from the road, yet it feels like another world. Pure, sweet air, fragrant with eucalyptus, floods my nostrils. A hush descends, as if the world is holding its breath to revel in the beauty of these stunning butterflies. I am spellbound. A butterfly brushes past my skin, and then it gracefully ascends and settles on a branch close to me, near another butterfly beating a single wing. I take a closer look and notice that this other butterfly is injured. I signal to Peter to come over.

"It's got a broken wing," he whispers. "That's one butterfly that won't make it to Mexico with the others." For some reason this comment sends a chill through me. How can life be so harsh? A butterfly injures its wing, and that's it. It's doomed.

Several minutes later, I find my voice again. "I've never seen these butterflies in South Africa. Their coloring – it's so lovely."

Peter turns around and walks toward the bicycles. "And so is yours."

"What?" My heart skips a beat. I gape at his back as I follow him.

"Your skin . . ." he murmurs, his back to me.

Just like that. "Your skin," as if he is talking about something ordinary like my shoes. My ears tingle, a little startled, to hear someone mention my skin so openly and loudly. No sly stares, or silly questions. Just a plain statement.

". . . reminds me of cinnamon . . . and nutmeg . . . and pumpkin pie . . . and spicy Christmas cookies . . . and . . . ." He stops abruptly, mounts his bike and rides away.

I gasp. I can't walk my bike all the way back home. "Peter?" He is out of earshot. I glower at my bicycle. How could he do this to me? Boy, is he in for an earful when I see him again.

In despair, I get on my bicycle, and roll it down, with one foot on the pedal, and the other foot dangling uncertainly. I recall Peter's encouraging words. "All it takes is self-confidence." Slowly, I bring my other foot onto the pedal and ride. The bicycle stays upright and I keep riding, tentatively at first, then gradually with more confidence. A smile spreads over my face. I can ride my bicycle now.

I pass Peter's house. He isn't anywhere in sight. As I ride home I shake my head and laugh. I'm on a high. I know it isn't just because I can now ride my bicycle.

I shake my head again thinking back to yesterday. *I've never seen anyone as attractive as you before.* Then today, he goes on about my skin, the most sensitive topic in the world, and the biggest surprise is I'm enjoying it all.

Chapter 10

I **rock my head and shoulders to the powerful** beats of Bongo Maffin as I help Mum put away produce we just bought at the Farmer's Market. Wendy, Stacy and I could never tire of this group for they are the absolute best performers of *kwaito* music, South African-style hip hop. We would dance and dance to their music on weekends until our feet literally couldn't hold us up anymore. *Kwaito*, with its pulsating dance beats, affects me in a way that no other music does. American hip hop does nothing for me. I only pretend to like it to avoid put downs.

Mum looks at me, shakes her head and mouths the words "Too loud." I turn down the volume on my portable CD player, my lips in a mock pout. After emptying out the last bag of veggies I dance to my room to work on my radio pen.

The progress I'm making on my invention has me floating on air. Then again, it could be any of the wonderful experiences of the past week that has me in this elated state—my growing friendship with Peter, making up with Chrystal and Jennifer, and discovering the pleasures of boogie boarding.

Yesterday, I had the most incredible time boogie boarding at Campus Point Beach with Chrystal and Jennifer. Thank God they forgave me so easily about the talent show business. I lean back on my chair, turn off Bongo Maffin, and relive my time at the beach.

The gentle, rocking motion of the water, and then the rising and cresting of the waves, my body, clinging to the boogie board, euphorically following the water's movement. Everything still feels so real— the brisk ocean breeze, the cries of sea gulls, even the outline of the nearby Channel Islands.

Yesterday I came to a realization about myself. The ocean is my first love, right alongside science (if it's possible to have two first loves). In Cape Town, I loved going to the beach and swimming in the Atlantic. By age four, I was a good swimmer and had no fear of the water. But since all the other kids seemed to love swimming too, I never thought about the ocean as having a special place in my heart. Yesterday, however, as I lay on my neon-striped boogie board, chemicals from inside me seeped into my veins, driving me into a state of total bliss. I knew then that I would never tire of the ocean.

Chrystal and Jennifer had to drag me out of the water. "If you think this is fun, wait till you try surfing," Chrystal commented, when she saw me beaming.

"I can't wait to start surfing." It all felt so dreamlike.

Thoughts about surfing and getting a surfboard jerk me back to the present. I've got to make this radio pen a reality. I know it'll make me a winner. So far I've managed to save $100 from my allowance. If I win the contest, I can easily buy a really nice used longboard.

I examine what I've done already and consider the next step. I've got to design a program to make the pen work. For this, Dad's new high-speed laptop, equipped with the latest operating system and software especially for research scientists would be perfect. But I'll need a clever excuse so he won't become suspicious about my secret. I could tell him I need it for a science report.

Instantly my stomach tightens. That dreaded ancestor report we're supposed to be working on. What am I going to do about that? I try to push it out of my mind. I'm about to get up and find Dad when Mum barges in. "Thandi?"

Oh no, I completely forgot. It's the evening we are spending at Ms. Moore's. I leap onto my bed and start groaning as if I'm in pain. The thought of facing Salif and Tasha and their probing questions makes it easy to fake agony.

"What's the matter, Thandi?" Mum's voice is filled with suspicion.

"I have a stomachache, Mum. Why don't you and Dad go without me?"

Mum walks over, pulls back the covers, and

rubs my stomach gently. "What's really going on? Did you not like Salif and Tasha?"

"I liked them."

"So, why are trying to get out of going?"

I shrug. Wish I knew the answer myself. "They're not my type," I mumble.

"Well, we have to learn to get along with all types," Mum says. "Up!" she commands. "We're leaving in a half an hour."

◊◊◊◊◊

The first thing I notice when we enter Ms. Moore's house is a huge painting hanging on the living room wall. It's an African wilderness scene painted on a piece of canvas that's shaped like an animal skin. Silhouettes of elephants and antelope frame a large lake. In the foreground are silhouettes of people in waist cloths, with baskets balanced on their heads. A deep orange background reveals a spectacular dusk. My eyes don't seem to want to leave the picture, even when Salif and Tasha come in to greet us.

The house feels immediately welcoming. Nina Simone's 'Strange Fruit' plays in the background. Because of Dad's passion for the old soul and jazz greats—American and South African—I've heard this music my whole life and can identify many songs after hearing just a few bars. A roaring fire crackles in the fireplace, and the air is thick with the fragrance of cooking herbs and spices. Ms. Moore, in a brown woolen dress, smiles broadly and holds out her hands to welcome us. "So good to see all of you. Come on in, Petrus and Nomse. Thandi, you look gorgeous in orange. Let me get your coats. Is it still raining?"

Mum and Dad start chattering away as if they are with old friends. "Oh, what a lovely living room you have, Carol." Mum's eyes glow with admiration.

Ms. Moore proudly tells us about the arts and crafts all over the room. She and her ex-husband enjoyed collecting unusual things while traveling in his native Kenya and its neighboring countries. Masks are mounted on the walls and huge clay pots and woven baskets line shelves. Standing on the mantelpiece are carvings of crocodiles, lions, rhinos, and giraffes.

"What an unusual coffee table," Dad comments as he examines the wood.

"That table is a treasure." Ms. Moore gently strokes the surface that shows the rings and knots of the tree from which it was cut. "Stinkwood. Got a real bargain," she murmurs, then crinkles her brows as if lost in a memory.

All during the drive to the Moores' house I was filled with dread. But right now, I feel like I've come back home after being away on a long journey. I feel faint stirrings from deep inside my body. Little goose bumps appear on my arms.

Salif and Tasha re-enter the living room just as the doorbell rings. "Ah, that must be Juliet and her mom," Tasha says, heading for the door.

"Juliet and Barbara are close friends of ours," Ms. Moore explains to us. "Barbara's been here all afternoon helping me make dinner. She left to change and bring Juliet over."

Juliet and her mother enter the house bearing a basket of fresh baked bread.

"Soul food was my pick for tonight's meal," Barbara says, after all the introductions. She is as tall as Ms. Moore, but has a softness to her. "When Carol told me you folks were from South Africa I said 'Carol, you must give them an authentic Southern meal.'" She lets out a hearty laugh.

Ms. Moore pats Barbara's shoulder. "And I said to her, 'Barbara, I'll need your help for that.' And, oh boy, did she help!"

"Let's go see what Juliet and Tasha are up to," Salif says to me. It's then that I notice the girls slipped away without even a word to me. A vein in my temple pulsates. I wish I had insisted on staying home.

Salif smiles at me. His dreadlocks are bundled in a ponytail, making his face look longer and his features more pointed. I look into his hazel eyes and see a maturity that both thrills and frightens me.

I follow him to a room where music is throbbing through the door. He knocks, then shakes his head. "It's Tasha's new Alicia Keys' CD. She's showing it off. Want to see my music collection?"

"Sure."

Salif's room is so full of stuff he has to push things away just to get inside. There are all sorts of musical instruments scattered about, books on the floor, his pajamas bundled on his desk, and CDs piled on his bed. On the wall hang two posters of a pair of handsome Black men. A well-dressed, distinguished-looking man in glasses graces one poster. At the bottom his identity is revealed: Malcolm X. The other poster shows a familiar-looking man, with a thin mustache and a goatee. His face expresses defiance and extreme self-confidence. No name appears on the poster, leaving me struggling to remember where I saw that face before.

Salif watches my gaze. "I bet you know who that is."

I shake my head.

Just then Tasha and Juliet burst into the room and fall onto Salif's bed. CDs clatter together. Tasha notices us looking at the poster. "Steve Biko, Salif's hero."

I know I've heard that name before but can't for the life of me remember when or where. Putting on a casual face, I ask, "Who is Steve Biko?"

Both Tasha and Salif gape at me. I shrink back.

"*Was* he," Salif corrects me. "Biko was a freedom fighter in *your* country back in the '70's."

I gulp. If he intended to make me feel dumb, he has definitely succeeded.

"Steve Biko started the Black Consciousness movement," Salif continues in a most teacher-like tone. "His message was similar to the 'Black is Beautiful' movement we had here in America in the '70's. Biko felt that Black people first had to work on their self-image before they tried to fight the apartheid government."

My face gets hot. Juliet saves me from the history lesson and further exposure of my ignorance.

"You don't have to go on and on, Salif. We get it. We know you know everything, okay." Juliet sits up and turns to me with an exasperated look. Her face is so different without her sunglasses. She has big, round eyes and thin, well-shaped eyebrows. In her short skirt, black tights, and high leather boots, she looks sexy, and older than a sophomore. "Salif can chew your ear off about politics."

Salif ignores her and looks at me. I pretend to be looking for a comfortable spot on the bed. "Steve Biko and Malcolm X are my heroes. Who are your heroes, Thandi?"

I chew my lips and gaze at each of the posters. What is the correct answer to this question? Salif's eyes are on me. I have to be honest or he'll see right through me.

"Scientists, inventors, people who have advanced our civilization. Darwin, Einstein, Newton."

"So your heroes are dead White men," he says accusingly.

I narrow my eyes at him, shocked that he too would be so petty as to think only in terms of White and Black. "You know, that's a silly way to look at life. We're all part of one race, the human race. Why should you only admire people who have the same skin color as you?"

"That's not the point, Thandi. Well, name some

Black scientists and inventors you admire."

Juliet growls. "Salif, why you giving her a hard time? You White like her too, you know."

Salif draws a deep breath and looks up at the ceiling. "And why, Juliet, am I being accused of being White?"

"You talk White, you go to them intellectual foreign movies, you hate rap music, want me to go on?"

"Juliet, don't you criticize my taste in music just because I refuse to listen to people disrespecting their women. Just look at my CDs. They're all Black artists, but most of them come from Africa. These are true artists who know about music. Most rap today is a disgrace to the concept of music."

I stare at his earnest face, impressed at his self-confidence. Why can't I have the guts to express my opinions so openly?

"You have such a closed mind, Salif," Juliet says. "What about Tupac? That brother understood what it means to grow up poor and Black in America. And he loved his people, man. Even did that song 'Dear Ma-'" She interrupts herself and turns to me. "You like Tupac's music?"

I know his music well. Wendy, Stacy, and I even saw the documentary about Tupac Shakur. But, I'm with Salif on rap music, even Tupac's. "Sure, I like him."

Juliet rewards my lie with a pleased smile.

"He also did the song 'I Get Around,'" Salif counters.

Tasha jumps up and straightens her skirt, which drapes beautifully on her lanky body. I notice prints of African wildlife near the hem. "Hey, I have an idea." She pulls her hair back and gives me a wink. "I bet Thandi would love some entertainment that comes from her continent."

"Now you're talking," Salif says, breaking into a cute smile. He gets behind the largest drum in the room, a conga. "You weren't serious the other day, were you?" he asks, turning to me suddenly. "About not knowing what tribe you belong to?"

I bite my bottom lip. With a shrug I say, "Well, when you grow up in the city, you don't pay attention to that stuff."

He gives me an unconvinced look. "That *stuff* is your identity. It's who you are."

"Half Xhosa and half Sotho," I force out, looking past him at the poster of Steve Biko. Why does he always make me feel guilty?

"Xhosa," Tasha murmurs, trying the word out on her tongue and practicing the clicking sound for the first syllable. "We don't have any Xhosa music in our collection. What's their music like?"

I shrug. "Don't know." The air feels heavy around me, almost choking me.

Salif starts beating his conga wildly. Tasha takes off her shoes and clears the floor. She hands Juliet a small, wooden drum. Then she gets behind some bongos. Salif points to a little talking drum and signals me to play it. Juliet nudges me. "Bet you had no idea you were coming to visit a couple of crazies."

She dumps the wooden drum on the floor and leaves the room.

Salif and Tasha have worked themselves into quite an energetic mood and urge me with their eyes to join in. I can't bring myself to do it. Frankly, I'd rather die than take part in this tribal behavior. It's the wrong direction for a California babe.

As I watch them, though, a funny thing happens. Those faint stirrings I felt earlier on, become stronger. Even though I can't bring myself to think it, I know that some part of me is enjoying the music of the African drums.

Suddenly I picture myself in Kheima, sitting around the fire with Granny and friends from the Xhosa village. During our visits, I used to sit glumly in one spot, tolerating the whole experience for Mum and Dad. I was of the city—modern, middle class and not at all interested in village life. On the drive back home from these visits, Mum and Dad would get into conversations about the joys of community living, and how these days more and more people have material comforts and fancy homes, but they don't even know their neighbors.

A realization dawns on me as I watch Salif and Tasha. The stirrings I felt earlier this evening, and now the emotions the drums evoke, they take me back to Kheima. Can it be that I actually *liked* going to Kheima?

Ms. Moore raps on the door. "Hey, quiet down there. That's way too loud, Salif," she scolds. "Anyway, it's dinner time." We follow her into the kitchen.

Freedom at last. I dive into my meal with a feeling of utter gratitude. Golden fried chicken, collard greens cooked in bacon, and fried sweet potatoes delight us all. Even Mum, the health freak, gorges herself. "The perfect meal for a chilly, winter's evening," she comments. Barbara, a bank teller, keeps us entertained with her hilarious stories about the neurotic people at her job. Unlike the prickly Juliet, Barbara radiates warmth.

After dinner, Tasha and Salif herd Juliet and me back to Salif's room. "You have to listen to some of my awesome music," he says to me.

"Listen to this. Baaba Maal from Senegal." Salif turns on the CD player. He rocks back and forth to the music. "Like it?"

"I do," I say truthfully.

"We'll have to drill you about South African music one of these days," says Salif.

Tasha jumps up and dances. Only it isn't a normal dance. It's like the dances of village people in Kheima. My mouth falls open. Juliet groans. "Why can't y'all two-step like everyone else?" She gets out her iPod and sticks her headphones into her ears. She flops on the bed and goes into her own world.

"I love African dancing," Tasha says to me. "Do you know any of the traditional dances from South Africa?" Her accent, which wandered back and forth from Black L.A. drawl to neutral all evening, is now neutral again.

My eyes pop wide open. "What?"

"Salif and I love doing the dances we learned in Kenya. They are the dances of the Masaai people. Want to see?"

Salif turns the music up and the two of them pound their feet on the floor, swing their hips, and then hop and kick their feet up, moving their heads and necks in rhythm, while throwing their arms about. I am astonished. The only people I ever saw dancing like this were people in Kheima dressed in cow hide skirts and decorated with body paint and tribal beads. We Cape Town middle class kids wouldn't be caught dead doing anything that looked so primitive.

"Come on, join in, Thandi." Salif beckons to me. "See if you can follow the steps."

I head for the door. Salif immediately switches the music off and grabs my shoulder. He gives me a funny look. "An African from Africa who knows nothing about being an African," he says.

"How dare you? You don't know me."

"You're right, I don't. But an oreo isn't hard to spot."

I could punch him. I could smash his precious CDs. I could scream a cuss word at him. But tears get in the way.

Tasha moves toward me. "You know, when Mom first told us about you, I was so looking forward to meeting you. I'm always thrilled to meet people from Africa."

"Why?" I surprise myself at how calm I sound.

"I just thought that a Black person from South

Africa would expose me to their culture. But you seem to know nothing. How come? Are you ashamed of your culture?"

I blink back tears. I can't talk. I wouldn't know what to say anyway.

"You know what my dad always tells us?" Tasha says. "He says we should see the world through African eyes."

I scrunch my face at her.

"Take a look at yourself, Thandi. You're an African, one hundred percent. But you are in denial. Too busy trying to be like White folks."

A hot tear rolls from my eyes. I bolt into the bathroom and more tears spill down my cheeks.

Chapter 11

*B*ack home the next morning I glare at the radio pen parts that I'm trying to connect together. Simmering with anger, I find it impossible to concentrate on my project. I can't get over how Salif and Tasha treated me last night. After telling me off and sending me fleeing to the bathroom, they just ignored me the rest of the evening. Luckily Mum needed to get back home to call her editor in Cape Town. I never felt a greater relief than saying goodbye to the Moores last night.

If I never see Tasha and Salif again, it will be too soon. It's fine for them to act all African. They aren't even from Africa. And Tasha, with her small cute nose and pretty pink lips, nobody is going to call her sausage lips. How dare she lecture me?

I try to stop thinking about them and focus on my invention. Deep breaths. If I succeed in creating this radio pen, no one will be insulting me anymore.

"Thandi," Mum calls. "It's Peter on the phone for you."

My heart does somersaults as I take the phone from her. I have no idea how he got my number, but I'm glad he did.

"Hi." My voice comes out husky from lack of use.

"Hey, Thandi. I was wondering, would you like to go bike riding?"

Peter's clear, actor-like voice sends me up to the clouds. "B-bike riding," I stammer. I look at the sky through the window. "I'm not sure. It looks like it's about to rain."

"It does? Oh, right. Well, want to come over for some chocolate chip cookies?"

I suppress the mega YES that wants to blast out. I need to be sensible about this. If I spend too much time with Peter, Jennifer and Chrystal are bound to find out about us. I can just say I'm busy. It won't even be a lie, because I really do need to spend every spare moment working on my radio pen. And since I'll be hanging out with Chrystal and Jennifer this afternoon, would it be wise to give up my morning too?

"Thandi?"

"Yeah, uh, sure, I'll come over for a cookie." It's the wrong response, but I rationalize to myself as I get ready, maybe spending a little time with Peter is just what I need after last night's episode with Salif and Tasha. I'm having trouble concentrating anyway, and I could use a boost to my mood.

The mood switch begins instantly. I hum a Bongo Maffin tune as I change from sweatpants to jeans and a warm sweater. I sashay along the sidewalk sucking in the fresh, moist air. The sky, a funny mixture of black, gray, and white swirls, seems so low I bet if I stood on a ladder I could touch it. Bright green grass carpets the rolling ground forming a nice contrast to the dull sky. A few cheerful orange poppies are beginning to poke through the grass.

Peter opens the door before I can knock. He greets me with his signature bashful smile. "Thandi, there's so much I want to show you," he says as he leads me in. "My room is up this way."

We walk through a dull living room, which has bare walls and exactly three pieces of furniture: two brown chairs and a coffee table. Then up a short flight of stairs and into a cluttered room. Peter looks far more relaxed than I've ever seen him and quite eager to show off his stuff.

He shows me different gadgets that he's made, or found in junk stores and modified. My favorite is a flashlight that you wear around your wrist like a watch. Each of its several buttons produces a different light intensity. Clearly, Peter is into science and engineering. I'm intrigued.

"Peter, I can't believe we're so much alike," I comment as I examine the books in his bookcase. He has a lot of the same books as I do, and quite a few I'd love to own. With increasing excitement, I read the titles: *Physics for the Young Mind, The Human Genome Project, Math Teasers, How Things Work,* and *Logic Anyone?*

All this science warms me, like a cup of

steaming hot chocolate on a chilly evening. None of my friends share my enthusiasm about science. It was the one interest that my Cape Town friends, Stacy and Wendy, and I didn't have in common. Jennifer and Chrystal get glazed looks when I bring up science. And here's Peter, somebody I didn't even want to be friends with, surrounded by the things I crave.

"Hey, is that your computer?" I ask, suddenly noticing a sleek grey laptop on a desk in the corner of the room.

"Uh-huh, but come on, let's go have some cookies, then we'll get on the Internet and I'll show you some neat web sites."

"You know, Peter, we sure have a lot in common," I say again as we scurry down the stairs to the kitchen. "My dad has been teaching me science and showing me how things work ever since I was in preschool."

"That's exactly the way my dad's been with me. Must be the way all scientists are."

An enormous antique table in the middle of the kitchen and a fireplace in one corner make the space feel cozy. We sit at the table and munch our cookies. "Peter, you've got to give me the recipe for these. They really are the best cookies I've ever eaten."

"Sure. Do you know, I've been making these since I was five years old?"

"Really? Your mom taught you when you were that young?"

"No, not my mom. It was Paulina." He gets quiet.

"Who was Paulina?"

He lets out a sigh. "Our housekeeper. She was like a mom to me when we were living in Louisiana. She'd appear in the morning, singing 'Jambalaya, and a crawfish pie, file' gumbo, 'Cause tonight I'm gonna see my ma cher amio,' and I would dive into her arms." His eyes are glazed. He's a little kid again. "She'd hold me close to her, and we would both dance and sing, 'Son of gun, we'll have big fun, on the bayou.'"

"I know that song," I say. We both break into song.

Jambalaya and a crawfish pie and file' gumbo
'Cause tonight I'm gonna see my ma cher amio
Pick guitar, fill fruit jar and be gay-o
Son of a gun, we'll have big fun on the bayou.

We look at each other and melt into laughter. My heart gives a jolt as our eyes meet. Then Peter becomes silent, and he fixes his eyes on the window. It's beginning to drizzle. Questions enter my mind. Where was his mom? Why didn't Paulina come with them to California?

"Peter, where are your parents?"

He looks at me, bites into a cookie, and says, "My parents? Oh, Dad's upstairs in his office." He takes another bite and says, "Paulina taught me to make all kinds of things. She used to say to me, in this very conspiratorial way, 'Always add cinnamon to cookies.' She was so funny. Cinnamon."

I grin, immediately thinking about my skin. "Hey, remember that day when you said all that stuff about my skin? What was that all about?"

Peter reddens. He stares into his empty cookie plate.

"Don't be embarrassed," I say, surprised at my own calmness on the topic.

He takes a deep breath. Then he tells me all about Paulina, a Black woman who took care of him while he lived in Louisiana. Paulina loved baking pies, especially pumpkin pie, and cookies, always adding spices like cinnamon and nutmeg to everything. "I loved the color of the spices. All those browns looked so beautiful to me. Then one time as Paulina was adding cinnamon to a pie, I noticed something amazing. It was the same color as her skin."

He pauses, then shakes his head. "I missed her for the longest time after we moved here." His mood turns somber. He absentmindedly piles more cookies on the plate. Then in a lowered voice, he says, "That day when you first walked into our classroom, I looked up, and . . . and I could smell Paulina's milk tart sprinkled with nutmeg."

I smile.

Suddenly, I feel his fingers on my hand. Slowly, he takes my hand in his and runs his thumb over it. "What a gorgeous color," he whispers. My heart stands still, and my breath comes out in soft gasps.

I love it. I love the feel of his hand on mine. But it's all so bewildering. I've never had a boyfriend before. I don't know what I should say or do. My eyes fall on our hands. I try not to be embarrassed at the contrast in our colors. After all, my dark color, makes Peter remember special things, a special person.

Peter takes his hands away and becomes his normal self again. "Hey, let's go back up to my room and check out my favorite website."

As he logs on, he says, "I suspected you were into science like me. That essay you wrote about the radio pen? Dead giveaway."

"Hey, I'm actually trying to make it," I blurt out, surprising both him and me.

"You are? Oh, come on."

"No, really, I am." Before I realize what I'm doing, I spill out all the details of my invention. His expression changes from surprise to confusion to disbelief.

"You're kidding," he says with a chuckle.

"I can show it to you if you want," I say, wondering why I have just confided a top secret to him.

"Well, then, forget about the Internet. I have some neat software I bet you'll really like. It helps you design electronic circuits for unusual gadgets." He inserts a disc into the computer and shows me how to use the program.

We try putting in different kinds of information and experiment with the outcome. Together we attempt to create a circuit for a talking calculator. But when we enter numbers and operations, the answer does not comes out in sound as it's supposed to.

"It isn't exactly easy," he explains. "But if we

keep at it, I know it'll work."

"Hey, could I bring my radio pen stuff over tomorrow and maybe we can try designing a circuit for it on your computer?" I ask, excited about this wonderful piece of technology. Maybe I won't need Dad's laptop after all.

"Sure, I'm dying to see it."

A deep voice interrupts our fun. "Peter, look what I found for your report." Peter's dad comes into the room without looking up from the piece of paper he's studying.

One look at him and I can tell right away why Peter is always weirdly dressed. His father has long, greying hair neatly combed in a ponytail. He's wearing a dark green vest, a clean, pressed white shirt, and black trousers. And his face is utterly strange—all creased—like he just sucked on a very bitter lemon. He doesn't notice me until Peter says, "Dad, this is my friend, Thandi."

"Oh," he says, looking startled and lifting up his glasses. "Nice to meet you, Thandi. Peter's been complaining about not being able to find anything nice about the Germans for his ancestor report. Well, here, son, I found some great stuff on a few classical musicians and some physicists."

"Thanks, Dad, I guess my report will have both good and bad things about my ancestors," Peter says, with a smirk. Then he looks at me and asks, "How's your report coming, Thandi?"

My hands ball up into fists. "I still have a ways to go."

Peter's dad looks at me and says, "I was telling Peter I'm really happy your teacher gave you this assignment. Roots are important. Plants need roots to keep anchored, and people are no different." He takes a deep breath, then says, "Well, it's lunchtime. Would you like to join us for lunch, Thandi?"

"Uh, no thanks. I have to go. My parents will be waiting for me." I hop down the stairs, grab my coat, and wave good-bye.

Even though I have my raincoat with me, I don't put it on when I get outside. I'm too warm from Peter's company to feel the chilly February air. My spirits are as high as the heavens. It's the first time since coming to California that I've felt so at home, so happy, with someone. I relive those moments when Peter's hand was in mine. I wish I could freeze that piece of time and live in it forever.

Too bad I can't tell Chrystal and Jennifer about Peter. When we talk about boys it would be so great to tell them how my heart dances when I'm with him. I sigh.

How weird that I have to keep my friends apart. What I get from Peter nobody else can give me. And what I get, what I need, from Chrystal and Jennifer, Peter can never give me.

I begin to muse, my thoughts changing as quickly as channels on a TV. Peter's stories about Paulina. Why does he not talk about his mom? Where is she? Peter's strange dad. His words ". . . roots keep plants anchored . . ." echo in my head. And that dumb ancestor report. What on earth am I going to do about that?

But my spirits are too high to let that assignment get me down. I do a zigzag skip all the way home, silently singing:

Jambalaya and a crawfish pie and file' gumbo
'Cause tonight I'm gonna see my ma cher amio
Pick guitar, fill fruit jar and be gay-o
Son of a gun, we'll have big fun on the bayou.

Chapter 12

Chrystal, Jennifer, and I are screaming along with The Spades.

> *It ain't my fault I ain't at work*
> *Can't you see, can't you see*

I'm dizzy with joy from my morning visit with Peter. I could sing forever, despite the rainy weather that sabotaged our plans to go boogie boarding. We're stuck indoors at Jennifer's house, yet the three of us, even Chrystal, are in high spirits.

The song comes to an end and Jennifer turns off the CD player. She smiles mysteriously. "Guess who asked me out to the movies?"

Chrystal squeals. "Let me guess. Let me guess. Ryan?"

Jennifer snorts. "Are you kidding? That walking ego? No way. I'm going to the movies next Sunday with—" she pauses for dramatic affect, "Tyler." She giggles and falls back on the sofa.

Chrystal's eyes fly open. "Tyler Hoffman?"

"I've had a crush on him since junior high." Jennifer nods and covers her face in embarrassment.

"And you've kept it a secret all this time? Out with it. We want details, don't we Thandi?"

"Yes, tell us everything," I say, feigning interest. I just want to close my eyes and think about Peter, his soothing voice and the gentle feel of his hand on mine only a few hours ago. Oh, what a dizzying sensation it was. Imagine how horrified these two would be if they could read my thoughts. I force myself to look at Jennifer and act excited.

"Well, I was at the Surf Shop on State Street yesterday browsing through stuff and there he was." Jennifer shrieks with excitement. "Right next to me looking at surfboards. When he saw me he smiled. Oh my God, he smiled. Then he asked, 'Do you surf?' I was so stunned I just stared at him, and then I nodded like an idiot and said, 'No, I'm learning. I'm still learning.' He said, 'Good for you.' Then he said, 'Did you hear about that new surfing movie that just came out? Waves of Joy?' And I said, 'Uh-huh.' And he said, 'Want to go with me to see it next Sunday?' That's right. Next Sunday!"

She screams as if she can't believe it herself.

Both Chrystal and Jennifer jump up, clasp palms and jig around the room. "I can't believe it!" Chrystal yells.

"I wish Ryan would ask me out," Chrystal says, turning somber.

"Ryan? Oh come on, Chrystal," Jennifer says, "you can do better than him. Ryan is so arrogant. Did you notice the way he walks to the basketball court? Like he's God or something."

Chrystal and I look at each other and smile. Only days ago Jennifer couldn't take her dreamy eyes off him. Chrystal scrunches her face at Jennifer, then stands up, stretches, and yawns. "Let's change the subject. I've got something to show you guys."

She unzips her bag. "I've got these really funny pictures for my ancestor report. Look." She giggles as she lays black-and-white photos on the floor. "This is my great grandma and grandpa. This picture was taken in Naples, Italy where they lived. This is my grandpa when he first came to America."

We crack up at the way her grandfather was posing in a pair of oversized shorts, long socks, and suspenders, smoking a pipe and leaning against a pole.

"And here's a picture of my grandma at her high school graduation."

"Is your dad actually allowing you to use those pictures?" Jennifer asks.

"Yeah, well, these are copies. He has the originals in an album," Chrystal replies.

"So how much more do you have to do on your reports?" Jennifer asks, looking at us both.

My fingers curl into fists.

Chrystal says, "Oh, I'm almost done. It's actually been really fun reading about Italian culture. And Dad's been helping me a lot too. What about you, Jen?"

"I've been a lazy bum. I downloaded stuff

from some websites and I have a bunch of books, but, well, I guess I should start on it. When's it due? We still have, what, three weeks, right?"

Chrystal nods and then they both turn to look at me. I'm biting my fingernails, pretending to be studying Chrystal's grandparents.

"How old were they?" I ask, not raising my eyes, hoping they'll forget I didn't say anything about my ancestor report.

"I don't know." Chrystal picks up the photo and stares at it for a few seconds. "Probably in their twenties. Hey, you guys, I have more pictures. Remember that day at Paradise Beach?"

Jennifer's eyes light up. "Oh, right, yeah."

Chrystal carefully puts away the photographs of her family and pulls out a fat envelope. The first photograph is of Jennifer in her skimpy two-piece swimsuit. She is lying on the sand striking a super model pose, with one hand running through her long, golden hair, and the other on her hip. The three of us gaze at the picture for a while. Chrystal says, "Jennifer, you should be a model." Jennifer smiles in appreciation of the compliment.

The second photo is of Chrystal holding Chloe in her arms. I smile at Chloe's sweet face, remembering our sand castle building. But, when she shows us the next picture my body goes cold.

Staring brutally back at me is the stark contrast. Ebony and Ivory. There's Chrystal and Jennifer, pale skinned and oh, so cute in their swimsuits, lying on the sand. And there's me, plunked between them. The voices of The Slugs thunder through me.

Sausage lips!

Midnight!

My stomach feels hollow. What are Chrystal and Jennifer thinking when they look at the picture of the three of us? Are they thinking, thank heavens we aren't dark like her?

But this morning's visit with Peter is still very fresh in my mind and waves of warm, nice feelings flow in and out of me, alternating with the embarrassment. It's like taking a shower and the water comes out hot and cold in turns. His voice rings in my head, his face dancing in front of me.

"Your skin reminds me of cinnamon . . . and pumpkin pie . . . I've never seen anyone as attractive as you . . . ."

I look at a picture of Chloe and me. When Peter sees my skin, he remembers something special. It's the *way* he sees me. I squeeze my eyes shut, then try to look at the picture again, differently. I could be beautiful, I guess. But, against my will, my eyes get pulled miserably to Chrystal's rosy cheek, which reminds me of the skin of a summer peach.

Jennifer gives me a huge nudge. She is shaking with laughter. "What? What's so funny?" I ask.

Between giggles she says, "You. You look ha, ha, so funny ha, ha, falling off the ha, ha, the boogie board." Chrystal and I take a look at the picture of me the first time I got on a boogie board and the three of us rock with laughter.

Chrystal frowns as she stares at a picture of

her and Jennifer. "You know, I hate my hair," she suddenly spits out. We both look up. "Look at this boring, straight hair," she whines, tugging at chunks of her dark brown hair, which she usually wears in a simple ponytail. "Maybe that's why nobody wants to ask me out."

Jennifer springs up and dashes out of the living room. She's back in a flash with a magazine. "Hey, my mom brought this from the hairdresser's the other day. Let's see if we can find styles we like. I'd like something more stylish too. Why don't we all get our hair done?" Her eyes are glowing. "Imagine, a whole new look." She spills out her sentences in strings like she always does when she gets excited, and runs her hands through her mane.

Beads of sweat settle on my neck and forehead as I watch Chrystal's face brighten. "Cool idea. Can you believe, I've never been to a hairdresser? My hair, it's always been long. Sometimes Linda gives it a little trim. But oh, this is such a great idea." She eagerly turns the pages of the magazine called *Styles Galore.*

I chomp my finger nails. This is a conversation I cannot join in. Black hair is a whole subject by itself only to be discussed by Black people, and even then it's touchy. I run nervous fingers through the springy coils on my head, which I've always hated. Chrystal can announce loudly to the world that she hates her hair. But me, I have to keep my feelings a secret.

"This style is so cool. I love it," squeals Chrystal. She points to a picture of a layered cut with the back swept out into a broad curl.

"Yeah, that will definitely suit you," Jennifer comments. "That style and a few new clothes would get all the boys competing for you."

I watch Chrystal as she frowns first at her plain jeans and sweat shirt, then at Jennifer's trendy, loose slacks and cropped black sweater. Two necklaces, a silver one, and a blue beaded one, and dangling blue earrings complete her look. I sigh with relief. In my wide, striped sweatpants and ribbed top, I definitely cannot be accused of lacking taste. Thank goodness for *Today's Teen.*

"That's mean, Jennifer," Chrystal snaps. "Not all of us get to live with our moms, and furthermore, not all of us have beauticians for moms, like you."

"Hey, girl, I'm only trying to be a friend. Your mom will get you anything you want. You should take advantage of that. I'm sorry if it sounded mean." She gives Chrystal a hug. "Let's get back to the magazine. I really, really want a new look." She stares at the picture that Chrystal pointed to earlier. "Hey, do you think this style will look good on me too?"

Chrystal moves Jennifer's head from side to side. Then she looks at the magazine again. "What about this one?" She points to a young woman whose hair starts out long at the front and gradually gets shorter, giving the bottom a sharp, angular slant. Chic is definitely the word that comes to mind.

Jennifer considers it for a few moments. "I like it. But do you guys really think it will look good on me?"

I smile picturing her in this drastically different look. "Of course, it will." I keep smiling, hoping my tone doesn't reflect the envy I feel.

Suddenly I can feel their eyes on me. I'm going to be sick. I can't talk about my hair. Plain and simple.

"What about you, Thandi?" Jennifer asks.

I cast my eyes down and laugh to hide my embarrassment. "Oh, I, my hair, uh, it's too short. Can't really do much." Sweat trickles down my forehead.

"That's crap," Chrystal says, turning the pages of the magazine. "Here are some styles for you. Look at this one. It says here it doesn't matter what kind of hair you have, or how short it is."

I take a look at the magazine. Pictures of Black girls with hair of various lengths in all different styles fill the pages. I gaze at the picture Chrystal is pointing to. There's a girl with her hair twisted into skinny braids.

"I'd need extensions for that. It would be way too expensive." My palms are drenched. I never dreamed I would ever be having a conversation about my hair and what to do about it with two White girls.

"Well, I bet we can find something different then," Jennifer says, peering at the pictures.

"I - uh, I don't know," I mumble. Mum and Dad would have a royal fit if I did anything fancy to my hair. Back in South Africa, Mum would often rant about poor Black women wearing scarves over their heads all the time because of the shame they felt about their hair. She found this very painful. And it infuriates her that so many urban Black women spend tons of money changing their hair because their natural hair is so utterly unacceptable to them. So whenever I've mentioned wanting to relax my hair, we ended up having huge blow-ups.

"Hey, Thandi To-mah-to, what do you mean you don't know?" Chrystal demands. "Do you want to be a California babe, or not?"

"Yeah, come on," Jennifer chimes in. "It'll be fun."

A chance to change my hated hair? Of course, of course, I want to do it. Maybe it's time to break free of Mum's control. It is my life after all. I look up at Chrystal and Jennifer and grin.

"Okay. Let's see what I can find in that magazine."

Chapter 13

It's the Saturday of our stylist appointments. I'm so excited that I've been up since 6 am. The morning seems to drag. I spend most of it working on the radio pen, making almost no progress. Peter and I have been working together on the radio pen every day this week. Since it's become a joint project, it is so much more satisfying to work on. We were making great progress until Thursday, when we encountered all kinds of glitches in programming the microchip.

Finding it hard to focus, I go into the bathroom and study my hair. I try to imagine how I'm going to look with permed hair. At $90 it's going to cost me practically all the money I've saved toward a surfboard. I groan at this setback. Then an idea dawns on me. Why not try and bum a few bucks from my folks? After all, my haircuts have never come out of my allowance.

I hear the doorbell and notice Mum going to get it.

"Oh, hello, Peter," I hear her say. "You'll find Thandi in her room."

Peter's brow is creased in thought as he enters my room. "I'm not going to give up until I get this thing figured out," he says in greeting. I smile at him, pleased that he has become so involved in a project that means a lot to me. Together we succeed in working out a different way to wire the devices. Now we have to test it on the computer using Peter's software. "Okay, Thandi, I'll input this new formula and let's see how it works. I think we're getting there."

Our eyes meet. My heart flips. "Thanks," I say, then, without thinking, I kiss him on his cheek. He smiles at me sweetly and turns beet red. My cheeks are flushed. I feel so light-headed, I'm surprised my feet can still hold me up. Peter turns to open his backpack. "I've been reading about South Africa." His voice is soft, tender.

I frown. "Why?"

"Well, because, it's where you're from. And I think it's one of the most wonderful countries on earth."

"You do?"

He shows me a book he's checked out from the library. "This book is about famous people from South Africa. I just finished reading about Shaka, king of the Zulus. Wow, he was an incredible leader. I mean to think that one man single-handedly created the mighty Zulu nation." His voice is filled with awe, and I want to hear more. How strange it is to feel utterly at ease, proud even, to talk about where I come from with someone.

Peter is different. He doesn't put me on the defensive. He doesn't make me feel self-conscious about my skin, or where I'm from. In fact, he has a way of making me feel fantastic about who I am.

"But Shaka was quite brutal," I point out. History books in South Africa make it very clear that cruelty was Shaka's most striking attribute.

"So were the European kings," Peter counters. "But Shaka's intellect would have put theirs to shame."

A silence falls between us. Then Peter clears his throat. "Are you busy this afternoon?" he asks.

I nod. "Jennifer, Chrystal, and I are going downtown." I keep my big event for today a secret. I want to surprise him. I want to see that smile of astonishment and admiration when he sees my new hairstyle. I mean if he thinks I'm beautiful now, wait until later today.

"I should go," he says. "Maybe I'll have good news about the radio pen tomorrow." Peter leaves, and I lie on the floor, dreaming about my lips on Peter's face. I can't believe I had the nerve to do it. Then I dream about the talent show, and me on stage showing everyone how Thandi's TelePen works. A glance at the clock shakes me back to reality. Almost time to meet Jennifer and Chrystal at Ben's Ice Cream. Anne, Jennifer's mom, will meet us there and take us to the hairdresser's, which is right next door.

But first, I have to scheme some bucks off my folks. I find Mum in the living room relaxed on the couch, singing the "Pata Pata" song along with Miriam Makeba. She never tires of her Makeba albums. On her lap lies Maya Angelou's *I Know Why the Caged Bird Sings*. I turn down the volume on the CD player and sidle up beside her on the couch. "Hey Mum, Dad says you have great news. What's up?"

"Ooh Thandi, you sound more and more Californian everyday." She grins. "Listen, darling, my editor and I spoke for a long time yesterday. He loved my story, *yebo*, and guess what? He wants me to write a novel. Ooh, mama, a novel! About our experiences, all of our freedom fighting in the '80's. Isn't that terrific?"

Her Xhosa accent leaps out at me and a tiny shudder goes through me. These days I've become so conscious of the way my parents talk. I feel like I want to correct how they pronounce their words. Maybe it's because everyone else I hear has an American accent.

"Sounds great, Mum, but when will you have time? Don't you always have weekly deadlines for the magazine?"

"Ooh, I haven't told you the best part." Mum's eyes shine with excitement. "I won't have to be doing any writing for the magazine at all while I'm working on the novel. So from now on, no deadlines. *Yebo!* Isn't that wonderful?"

"Yes, it is wonderful. Mum, I was wondering, can I have money for a haircut?" I wrap my arms around her, taking advantage of her good mood.

She pulls away to look at me and holds my

chin up. "Hmmm, your hair is looking quite bushy. You could definitely use a trim."

She hands me a $20 bill. "Do these hairdressers do Black people's hair?"

"Yeah, they do."

"Need a ride there?"

"Oh, no. We're going to the one at the shopping center just up the street. I can bike there."

I slip the bill in my pocket and go in search of Dad. He is in the spare bedroom that he and Mum use as an office. I knock quietly. "Dad, I need $20. I'm going with my friends to that shopping center up the road. I need money for uh—um a haircut."

He doesn't look up as he reaches into his back pocket and gets out his wallet. After a quick glance at the bills, he pulls out a twenty, hands it to me absent-mindedly, and turns back to his work.

Phew! That went way easier than I expected.

I ride up the road to the shopping center, quite nervous about what I'm about to do. After securing the lock on my bicycle, I skip into Ben's. As I look around for Jennifer and Chrystal the woman behind the counter calls out in a grumpy voice, "What do you want?" She scowls at me.

"I - I'm waiting for my friends," I stammer.

She purses her lips, and shoos me outside with eye motions, while pointing to the door. Jennifer and Chrystal appear just as I step outside.

"I can't believe what I'm about to do!" Jennifer squeals, her face full of smiles. I get behind them as we enter, expecting more grouchiness from the woman.

Instead, she smiles at them sweetly. "Hi, what

can I get you?"

"I'll have chocolate on a sugar cone with one topping of M&M's," Jennifer says.

"I'll have vanilla on a waffle cone with strawberries and nuts, please," Chrystal says.

"Great. That will be ..."

"Wait, what about her order?" Jennifer asks, pointing to me.

Standing behind Chrystal and Jennifer and watching the woman take no notice of me, I realize exactly what's going on. How often in my life I've experienced this. This feeling of being invisible when I'm the only Black person among a group of Whites.

"Oh, she's with you?" the woman asks, looking surprised. She turns to me, and asks, "What will you have?"

"The chocolate, with M&M's," I say to the counter. It takes effort not to shout my order at her.

When the three of us sit down, Chrystal frowns. "That was weird, her not noticing you, Thandi."

"Not to me. It's all part of the Black experience." I feel nowhere near as cool about it as I sounded. I look enviously at their faces, so creamy, so like the faces in *Today's Teen*. Guilt trickles through me for my forbidden thoughts.

I watch the small frowns on their faces as they lick their ice cream. I try to rehearse answers to questions I expect them to ask, but they say nothing. Then, as if shrugging off the intimacy I just shared with them, they turn to each other and chat about the new hairstyles we're going to have. "I can't wait to see Tyler's face tomorrow," Jennifer squeals.

My head droops. I feel like a kid taken to a candy store only to be told she can't buy anything. I'm homesick. My mind and body separate. My body is still there, but my mind goes to Stacy and Wendy in Cape Town. "What a dumb, ignorant goat!" Wendy sputters, and they both make faces and gestures whenever the woman turns away, doing everything to show that I'm okay and the woman is not.

A seed of doubt floats about, finds a spot in my heart, and settles down.

Chapter 14

Chrystal lets out a shriek of delight. "Wow! I love my hair! I love it!" She does a jig in front of the mirror at the salon. I stare enviously at her beautifully-layered silky hair tapering around her shoulders and curled out at the back.

Jennifer is quietly studying her own new hair. Her blond mane is parted in a zigzag in the middle, then falls in an arc, long and uneven on both sides and short at the back. She looks even more gorgeous than before. Anne smiles. "You look great, Sweetheart."

My blood is boiling with fury as I sit and let the stinky, white cream the hairdresser put into my hair, do its job. Even though Stella, my stylist, warned me about the pain, I wasn't prepared for it to be this bad. My scalp feels like a piece of steak on a barbecue grill. My nostrils and lungs are clogged with sharp, acid-like fumes.

It's so unfair that Jennifer and Chrystal didn't have to experience anything uncomfortable at all.

Instead, they get to watch me go through my ordeal. My insides churn and the ice cream I ate earlier ejects from my stomach and into my throat. Sharing the excitement before getting our new hairstyles was one thing. But sitting here in the salon, me watching their straight, long tresses snipped into dainty styles, while they witness my springy coils being bullied into hair that looks like theirs, is just plain humiliating.

"Listen, Honey," Anne says to me, "We're going over to Kmart. Be back in a little while, okay?"

I nod. I can't blame them for not wanting to wait. It's been an hour and I'm not even half-way finished. I sit back in the chair and continue my wait.

"All done, Thandi," Stella finally says, more than two hours after it all started. "It's taken well. What do you think?" she asks with a pleased grin. Stella's hair cascades down to her waist. "I'm lucky. I have good hair," she told me earlier when I asked her about the relaxing process. "Never needed chemical treatments. That's why it's so healthy."

I gaze into the mirror both shocked and thrilled by what I see. A sleek, chin-length bob frames my round face. I toss my head. There's a ticklish, fuzzy feeling on my neck. I turn back to the mirror and run my hand through my hair. The softness sends shivers of joy through me. Stella indulges my desire to ogle and holds up a hand mirror so I can see my new style from all angles. Gosh! I look so...different!

"Now girl, I'm going to give you some advice. Sister to sister advice," Stella says. She pulls up a chair and sits beside me. "First of all, you must be sure to use good hair care products. I've got a list to give you. Moisturizing is real important. Dry hair is our big problem. But after chemical treatments, it's an even bigger problem. Keep that hair moisturized, girl, or you'll be sorry. Drink lots of water. Lots of water. It really helps. Do you wear a silk scarf at night?"

I nod.

"Good. And remember no hot combs. Not on relaxed hair. They'll burn your hair right out. What kind of comb do you use? Wide tooth?"

"Uh-huh."

"And you know to comb from the end up?" She tugs a lock of my hair and demonstrates.

"From the end up?" I ask, a little confused.

"Uh-huh. You comb this way," she says, repeating her demonstration.

"Oh, yes. I know. That's what I always do."

She reaches for a notebook, flips through it, and pulls out a yellow sheet. "Here's a list of good hair care products that I recommend. The shampoos and conditioners from this company are great. They have a hair oil blend too."

"Thandi To-mah-to, you look fab!" Chrystal grins at me, as she, Jennifer, and Anne enter the salon. Each of them holds a Kmart shopping bag.

Jennifer and her mom nod in agreement. "It's gorgeous," Anne says.

As I cycle home, doubts about whether my new hairstyle suits me float in and out. Then the thing I'd been avoiding all week confronts me full on.

My parents! How am I going to prevent them from completely freaking out? I rehearse different stories as I approach my home.

"Hi Mum. New hairstyle? What new hairstyle?" Faking surprise, I step toward a mirror. *"Oh my gosh! You're right!"*

"Hey, Mum and Dad, recognize me? I only look like a movie star. Actually I'm a scientist."

"Mum, Dad, look what my friends made me do?"

"The hairdresser did that. I think she couldn't hear me. But, do you like it?"

"I said I wanted a haircut. She showed me all these pictures and asked which one I liked and I chose this one. Like it?"

At home, Dad is in the kitchen humming a tune. I stand outside the back door gathering up courage to enter the house. A scrumptious aroma of something baking, probably scones, wafts through the door. Okay, which story is it going to be? I take a deep breath, put on a smile, turn the handle, and enter.

"Hey, Sugar, where . . ." Dad begins, and then freezes when he sees me. His face twists into an expression that makes my heart thump against my ribcage. "Wh - What did you do to your hair?" he yells.

"I - I —"

"Go. Go to your room, young lady."

Standing in front of the mirror in my bathroom, I examine my reflection, while bracing myself for my parents' fury. With a pounding heart I try to go over the stories I thought up earlier. But, of course, I know they aren't going to buy any of those excuses.

I turn my face to the left, then to the right, up, and then down. I make different expressions, a Mona Lisa smile, a wide, happy smile, a frown, a look of shock. Yes, I think I'll like my new hair once I get used to it.

But, how much trouble am I in?

The door flies open. "THANDI! THANDI!" Mum's bellows make the floor vibrate.

I slowly creep out of the bathroom, my head bowed and my hammering heart knocking against every cell in my body.

"WHY? What . . .? Why . . .?" she yells.

"Mum, w-w-why, why, are you so angry?" I barely manage to stammer the question.

"Why am I angry? You want to know why I am angry? I'll tell you why."

Her flaming eyes make me shrink back. I want desperately to duck and cover. This is worse than an earthquake.

"A. You were dishonest. You said a haircut. You wanted $20 for a haircut. Why didn't you tell me the truth? B. You are only fourteen years old. What makes you think you can make such major decisions about your appearance by yourself? C—"

"Wait," Dad butts in, as he appears in my doorway. "Didn't *I* give you $20?"

They look at each other and then at me. My eyes dart around searching for an escape. I'm caught, tried, and about to be convicted. They are going to kill me. I just know it.

By some miracle, the doorbell rings. Dad goes to get the door. "Hi, is Thandi home?" When I hear Peter's voice, I march out to the living room. "You have five minutes with Peter," Mum shouts out, "and then you have some explaining to do."

When Peter sees me, his mouth falls open. Then he frowns. "Why did you do that?"

I shrug. "Do you like it?"

"Not really. I liked it the way it was. You're one of those girls with natural beauty."

I am irritated at his reaction. Compounded by what I just went through with Mum and Dad, I feel mean-spirited. I want to yell, "what would a geek like you know about hairstyles?" It takes all my energy to keep myself under control.

Peter clears his throat and gets all business-like. He kneels beside the coffee table and lays out the parts of the radio pen. "Hey, this is going to work great. So, I figured out that for the transmission we'll need to use an infra-red light, because we're passing messages remotely. The light picks up the signal, sends it to the computer chip, and the receiver gets the message. What do you think?"

I'm in such a state of turmoil that nothing he says makes sense to me. "Amazing." It seems like an appropriate comment. "Uh, Peter, could you do that part for me?"

"Oh, sure. I just thought I should tell you the great news. Okay, I've got to go. See you tomorrow," he says robotically.

No tender smile. Is it because of my hair? Not that I care, anyway. I mean, how dare he not have the good manners to rave about my new hairstyle?

And suddenly I'm shaking with fury. It's my life. Why is everyone trying to control it?

After Peter leaves, Dad, followed by Mum, stomp into the living room. I glare at my parents for it suddenly becomes clear to me. They are control freaks. How is it I haven't seen it before? "Don't you think you guys are overreacting? I got my hair relaxed. What's the big deal?"

Dad draws in a breath and shakes his head. "And I thought we raised you to take pride in who you are."

Mum glowers at me. "I can't believe you've ruined your beautiful hair."

I stand straight up and put my hands on my hips. "Beautiful?" I scream. "Mum, let's face reality. There is nothing beautiful about our hair!"

She slumps down on the couch with a gasp, glaring at me.

"Thandi, get to your room now," Dad commands in the iciest, sternest tone he's ever used on me. "And stay there until we've thought of a suitable punishment."

Tears fill my eyes, but I force myself to stay composed. "Mum, Dad, I have news for you. Parents don't own their kids." Then I flee to the safety of my room. Inside my belly is a volcano ready to erupt.

So I was wrong to deceive them about my hair.

But, what choice did I have? They never would have agreed to it. I know them well enough to know they wouldn't understand why I have to embrace a new image. It's all well for them to preach about the stupid natural look. They are too wrapped up in their careers to notice the real world.

Hot tears, like flaming lava, spew from my eyes. My insides clench. For the first time in my life there is a very real barrier, a wall, between my parents and me.

Chapter 15

*A*ll the freshman biology students of our school are assembled in the auditorium on this cold Tuesday morning. Dad is about to do his presentation. I watch him organize his transparencies. It's been three days now since the blow-up over my hair, and the tension at home remains high. As I brush back strands from my forehead, I wonder how Dad and Mum can be so proud of being part of 'The Struggle' in the '80's in South Africa, yet know so little of their own daughter's struggle taking place right here and now.

Dad starts his presentation by showing the class his diving gear and equipment. Excitement ripples through the audience. "Who would like to try on some of this equipment?" Eager hands shoot up. He picks one student from the back and one from the middle. Loud groans of disappointment rumble across the room.

After the equipment demonstration, Dad turns

on the slide projector and shows us slides of sea creatures in the ocean around Cape Town. Everyone seems fascinated, all eyes glued to the screen that displays an enlarged picture of an unusual red fish with a spiky dorsal fin. Dad tells the class that even as a child, of all the animals he learned about, he found fish the most interesting. He describes the habits of a fish named a jacopever that's pictured on the screen. All I hear is his strong accent. It makes me cringe.

Suddenly the sound of tittering distracts me. I turn automatically to see where it's coming from. A twinge pricks my stomach. Those moronic slugs.

With mischievous grins, they exchange whispers and snickers. I strain to hear what they're saying. My ears get hot and I crack my knuckles. I should have guessed. Dad's accent.

What happens next is even more humiliating. Chrystal and Jennifer, sitting beside me, with Nate and Matt on the other side of them, join in.

"Uhnimals," one of them mutters, mocking Dad's pronunciation, and the others burst into giggles.

"Lehhned," another imitates.

I give Jennifer and Chrystal a confused glance, then look down at my sneakers. The seed of doubt in my heart sprouts a tiny root.

Then my mind spins out of control. A combination of forces pull me: the anger from Saturday burning in me; my desire to be like Chrystal and Jennifer; the unfair punishment of being grounded for two weeks; and a new annoyance toward Dad.

Why does he have to have such a dumb accent? I lean toward Chrystal and Jennifer.

And I join in.

Dad shows us a diagram on a transparency and I imitate him under my breath. "You cuhn see the feen is beeg uhnd wide." Nate, Matt, Chrystal, and Jennifer are in hysterics. Other kids turn to look at us.

Dad glances in our direction and pauses for a few seconds, his eyes now directly on me. I see a twitch of his left cheek, a wince, as if he just got stung by an insect. My fingers fly to my left cheek, nursing an imaginary sting. Then, Dad is back to his presentation.

Mrs. Miles, our biology teacher, marches up to us, and gives us a stern "Hush!" I turn to look at her and notice Peter glaring at me with a fierce frown.

My heart knots up. The wall between my parents and me feels higher, thicker. I feel lost, alone.

Dad continues with his talk, pausing to listen to questions, and then answering with total ease and confidence. When he's done, everyone applauds enthusiastically. He gathers up his things and leaves the auditorium.

Mrs. Miles begins a discussion on Dad's presentation. "Questions? Comments? What did you learn?" She selects a marker, pulls off its cap and is ready to write on the board.

Matt raises his hand. "My question is, why does Professor Sobukwe say *uhnimuhl* instead of animal?" The class explodes with laughter.

I pray for the floor to open up and swallow me.

My forehead is drenched in a sweat. I look around, hesitate for a few seconds, then my mouth takes on the shape of laughter. And the sound that leaves my lips is like the laughter from a wind-up toy.

Suddenly Peter springs up and yells, "You are all so immature!" Stunned silence fills the room.

Jennifer nudges me and with a smirk, mumbles, "And Mr. Britannica is so mature."

Mrs. Miles clears her throat. "Thank you, Peter, for your observation." She looks around the room, shaking a disapproving head. "I am shocked at you guys. Making fun of someone's accent is extremely disrespectful. And especially someone as distinguished at Professor Sobukwe."

"But Mrs. Miles," one of the students, Richard, protests, "we weren't laughing at the professor. We were laughing at Matt's question."

I feel numb as I watch the dumpy Mrs. Miles walk back toward the board. "Okay, let's hear some sensible comments or ideas about the presentation."

The image of Dad's flinch haunts me.

The class falls into a more serious mode and in a few minutes the board is filled with information gleaned from Dad's presentation. The bell rings and Mrs. Miles assigns us a report on Dad's presentation for homework.

Then she looks up and calls out, "Nathan, Matthew, Jennifer, Chrystal, and Thandi, I'd like a word with you. The rest of you are dismissed." In a curt voice she says, "You five will write a letter of apology to Professor Sobukwe. Your behavior during the presentation was unacceptable."

Unacceptable.

Discomfort jostles with anger, wins over, then turns into shame, regret.

Jennifer, Chrystal, and I head for our lockers. Chrystal snickers. "Uhnimuhl," she mocks.

I bite my lips, keeping my head down.

"The feen of the feesh," Jennifer says.

"That Mister Britannica," Jennifer suddenly says as we walk away from our lockers. I shut my eyes and hold my breath.

"Yeah," Chrystal says. "What's with his superior attitude?"

"You know, have you ever spoken to Peter?" I sputter.

They roll their eyes back as they turn to look at me. "No," Jennifer says. "Why would I want to speak to someone so weird?" She tosses her chic hair in a snobby manner. She's been doing this ever since her haircut on Saturday. I find it irritating.

"Well, if you haven't spoken to him, how can you say he's weird?" I ask.

Chrystal snorts. "Oh, come on, Thandi. You know what we're talking about. Look at the way he dresses and talks. And he always keeps to himself. He thinks he's too smart ..."

"Excuse me." It's Peter. He appears from behind, his frown now fiercer. My heart stands still. "Thandi, I just want you to know, we aren't friends anymore. You are not the person I thought you were." And he storms past us.

Chrystal and Jennifer gape at me as if an alien just fell from the sky and landed in front of them. Me, I'm shaking, shaken. A moment's hesitation, confusion, then I bullet after Peter.

"No, wait," I shout. "Peter, no, please—" He turns around and says, "And I won't be helping you on the radio pen." He keeps marching away, ignoring my protests.

An avalanche of rocks tumble down, engulfing me, isolating me from everyone, everything.

The monarch butterfly with the injured wing flashes in my mind. The one that won't make it to Mexico this year.

Chapter 16

Dad's car is in the driveway when I get home. I summon all my strength and enter the house. He's in the living room reading the *New York Times*. It's a normal scene as if everything is okay. A flicker of hope. Maybe he didn't see me making fun of him. Maybe he's even forgiven me for relaxing my hair. "Hi Dad!" He looks up and cold, dark eyes squint at me.

I swallow the bitter taste that comes into my mouth. The menacing wall between my dear dad and me looms large. "Dad, your presentation was fantastic." Ignoring me, he turns back to his paper. I walk away to my room saying, "Dad, I'm sorry." My voice sounds unnatural, laced with shame. He remains silent.

I slink up to my room and throw myself on the bed. Huge sobs from the deepest depths of my being rack my body. This has been the absolute worst day of my life. What have I done? How did I manage to turn everyone against me?

The walls in my room seem to close in on me. I quietly creep out, and get on my bike. Being grounded has always meant not being able to hang out with my friends. My parents can't object to a bike ride.

I ride around aimlessly. A few monarch butterflies hover around me. I glance to the side and notice the towering eucalyptus trees bordering the butterfly grove. I get off my bike, lean it against a tree, and enter the grove.

All at once a calm enters my body. My skin soaks up the peace and quiet that surrounds me, like a thirsty sponge. A rock with a flat top beckons me to sit down. Shafts of sunlight beam through the branches. The air smells fresh, perfumed with a mixture of damp earth, ocean saltiness, and pungent eucalyptus. I hear a faint hum from the fluttering butterflies. Their flaming orange wings, streaked with bold black lines that seem to follow some complex pattern, glow in the slanted rays.

As I gaze at the butterflies I ache for things to be right between me and Peter again. I remember so clearly everything about that first time he showed me this place. What a special time that was. I sigh.

Thoughts, messages, voices bombard me from all directions. Like the thousands of monarch butterflies flitting around, my head is buzzing. Nate and Matt. Jennifer and Chrystal. California babe. Peter. Salif and Tasha. Mum. Dad. African eyes. Cinnamon. Kheima. Granny. I clasp my palms and press them under my chin, staring at the sudden movements of butterflies resting on a branch.

Tasha's voice echoes through me over and over again. *Dad always says we should see the world through African eyes.* I wonder what that means. Where are my African eyes? Can a California babe have African eyes?

Steve Biko's face, filled with self-confidence, focuses in my mind.

Then my thoughts bounce to Chrystal and Jennifer. Them teaming up with The Slugs to make fun of Dad. Me teaming up with them.

My dad. His disappointment in me.

Mum. *My hair is part of my identity. The identity for which we risked our lives fighting.* These are words she has uttered to me many, many times.

With a heavy heart, I slowly cycle back home. My mind is muddled, my heart in torment, but strangely there is one thing I become acutely aware of. Thandi's TelePen is not the answer to my problems.

◊◊◊◊◊

It's late, probably past midnight, but I can't get comfortable in bed. I keep pulling the covers, I toss and turn, but my body refuses to fall into a relaxed state. Everything that happened yesterday keeps popping into my mind in jumbled frames, like a movie out of sequence.

The house is deathly quiet. A full moon casts a silver light on my bed. I sit up and gaze at the bright orb. I peer into the telescope that's affixed to a stand near my window. Venus and Jupiter twinkle beside it, and the constellation of Orion is proudly outlined against a mass of inky satin. A distant howl. Coyotes.

I sink back under the covers and try to fall asleep. Gradually my breathing becomes deeper, heavier and . . .

Noise. Laughter. I'm sitting in front of a birthday cake, candles all aglow. Everyone, Chrystal, Chloe, Jennifer, Tess, Erin, Richard, and a few others from my class are around the table. I blow out the candles. Everyone claps and cheers.

I need to use the bathroom. As I walk down the hall, I hear crying behind a closed door. I turn the handle, open the door and see Granny sitting on a chair, hands over her face, weeping. She has a Xhosa blanket draped over her shoulders, and there's white paint on her face. I walk up to her. "Granny, Granny, what's wrong?" I ask.

She shakes her head. "Why won't you let me come to your party?" She has a look of deep sorrow.

"They'll laugh at you. Your clothes, the way you talk. They won't understand you."

"It's up to you, Thandi. *You* make them understand."

I put my arms around her, and cry, "How?"

A coyote howls. My eyes open. Moonlight floods the room. Just a dream, thank goodness. I wrap the covers closer around me and try to fall back to sleep.

Chapter
17

African eyes. African eyes. The words buzz through me as the darkness melts away. I jump out of bed even though it's only 6 a.m. Like the White Rabbit in *Alice in Wonderland* who has to find his kid gloves, I feel the same urgency to find my African eyes.

A surge of energy flows through my veins. Last night, I felt helpless. But now, as dawn breaks, things that I simply must do become crystal clear, filling me with a fiery strength.

I'm up and at my desk. I need markers and a small piece of white paper. The South African flag has more colors and is more complicated than other flags, but I know it by heart. Blue, white, green, red, yellow, and black. A lot of colors to cram into a teeny space. The middle part houses the colors of the African National Congress, the political party of my parents—green for the land, yellow for the gold, and black for the people.

Next I turn on the computer and send Peter an e-mail message:

Dear Peter,

How do I even begin to express how sorry I am about yesterday? I am ashamed of my behavior. I don't think I need to tell you how special you are to me, and how deeply I value your friendship. Please forgive me.

Sincerely,
Thandi

Morning noises indicate my folks are up. I get ready for school.

In World History class, I attach a toothpick to my miniature flag and poke it into the big world map right where Cape Town is. A solitary flag at the bottom of a huge continent. The only flag in the southern hemisphere. Asia displays a lonely flag too. Philip Kojima's ancestors are from Japan. Two flags fly in Mexico and lots of flags in Europe.

Jennifer is absent today. Chrystal, to my surprise, catches my eye while we are working on a worksheet. And I was so sure that after yesterday's drama they wouldn't want to have anything more to do with me. I turn away. I need some time to think about my friendship with Jennifer and Chrystal.

Between classes, I wander off to the lower field. I sit on a bench and watch a ladybug crawl into a little flower. "Hey." It's Chrystal. Didn't take her any time to find me.

"Thandi," she murmurs. "I'm sorry about yesterday. Your dad . . ." She's in low spirits today.

I nod. Then, changing to a demanding tone, and flapping her palms, she asks, "What's going on with you, Thandi? You are friends with Mr. Britannica and you don't tell us. And what's this surprise you have for the talent show?"

"Chrystal." I sigh. "I can't talk about it. There's just too much to think about right now."

"I can't believe you were friends with Peter. What got into you?"

I glare at her. "You want to know something? Becoming friends with Peter is the best thing that's happened to me in California."

She grimaces—as if she's just swallowed some bitter medicine. "What? But, he's so—out there!"

"You don't know him, Chrystal. You've never spoken to him. Peter is so smart and sensitive. I guess life hasn't been easy for him." My voice chokes up. I turn away from Chrystal and stare at the craggy mountains etched against a dull sky. I screwed up. Peter and I may never again have what we had.

"What do you mean?" she demands.

I shrug. "Well it can't be easy—just him and his dad."

"Where's his mom?"

"Don't know."

Her face takes on an expression of great curiosity. I can tell that the information has struck a nerve in her.

The bell rings for third period. As we walk to Algebra class, I decide to express the thought that's been going through my mind all morning. "Chrystal, I don't think I can be friends with you and Jennifer anymore."

She gives me a puzzled look. "Why? I said I was sorry about teasing your dad."

I shake my head. "It's much more complicated than that, Chrystal. I need friends who respect me and everything about me." My courage surprises me.

"But I do," she protests.

"If you did, you wouldn't put Africa down the way you and Jennifer do every time the topic comes up." Her befuddled eyes study me as if she's seeing a whole new person.

That's right. A lot can change in a few days.

◊◊◊◊◊

When I get home from school, I empty my backpack and hand Mum a flyer from Mr. Roth inviting parents to our ancestor presentations in about two weeks. Mine is slightly different from everyone else's because when Mr. Roth was passing out the flyers, I explained to him that I wanted the topic to be a surprise to my parents. He smiled, went to the computer, hit a few buttons, and out came a special copy for me in which the words "World History" were substituted for "Family Ancestry and Heritage" and the part about bringing a dish representing our heritage deleted.

Mum takes the flyer without looking at me or saying anything. Four days since Saturday and she's still mad. All day today I've been thinking about a plan to set things right between us.

Time to get started on this plan. I sling my empty backpack over my shoulders, tell Mum where I'm going, then pedal down the road. My destination is the public library. A cheerful librarian guides me to the nonfiction section when I ask for books about South Africa.

Just one full shelf is devoted to the entire continent of Africa and its people. Straightaway I find five or six books that look promising. One, titled *Children's First Book of Africa*, is meant for younger readers, but it looks like it contains information I might be able to use. Another is about Southern Africa, and there's one specifically about South Africa.

When I go to check out my books I suddenly think about Steve Biko again. That look on his face that ensures you can always feel safe with him has been popping in my mind a lot recently. "Ma'am, I was wondering if you have a book about Steve Biko?"

"Let me see," she says, punching something into the computer. Then she walks over to a shelf and brings back a book. "This is the only one we have. It's a collection of Biko's writings."

"Thanks." I check out the books and head back home.

After dinner, I go to my room and browse through the books. When I open up *Children's First Book of Africa* I'm immediately hooked. Hungrily, I take in page after page of fascinating information about Africans across the continent. The wealthy, gold-rich kingdoms of Ghana, Mali and Songhay. Great universities, such as the one in Timbuktu with one of the largest libraries in the world, built before European countries had universities. Important civilizations in places like Benin and Kilwa. Great temples and mosques built before European explorers set foot on the continent. Today the ruins still stand. How intriguing!

Dad sticks his head into my room. "Past your bedtime, Thandi." His voice is cool. He doesn't come in to give me a good night kiss or to sit down for a little chat like he used to do. To see Dad, my best friend, so mad at me, hurts worse than The Slugs' taunts. I stare at Dad's retreating feet, determined to make things right again between us.

I brush my teeth, get into my pajamas, and creep under the covers. As soon as I close my eyes, pictures from a book I was reading earlier pop into my head. I'm dying to read more. The book lies on my bedside table, tempting me, like an ice cold drink on a blistering day.

Just a few more pages, I think. . .

I can't stop reading when I get to the part about the Xhosa. A feverish excitement consumes me. Reading about these people who were extremely close to nature in a land blessed with immense beauty, fills me with a warm glow. Working on the radio pen was fun, but learning about my ancestors is like food for my soul. Considering how I've always scorned tribal living, my reaction is a total surprise to me.

I picture Mum when she was a kid running around in the open fields of Kheima among the cows and goats, going to a one-room school, helping Granny fetch water every evening, and sleeping in a mud hut. My life in Cape Town, and now in Buena Vista, on the other hand, is so different. So western. Mum sees the world from an African point of view because of where she grew up. In fact, she rejoices in her African identity.

That's it! That's what it must mean to have African eyes. But unlike Mum who probably was born with African eyes, I have to search for mine.

Chapter 18

*M*um shakes me awake, but my eyes want to stay shut. I try to force them open. Ow! They burn. "Thandi, are you okay?" Mum looks concerned. She puts her hand on my forehead to see if I have a temperature. "It isn't like you to still be in bed on a school morning."

I force my lips apart. "I . . . I think I didn't get . . . much sleep." The words are barely audible.

Mum pulls the covers over me again. "I'll call the school. You should stay home today. You're probably coming down with something."

I close my eyes, and as I fall asleep again, images from the books I was reading last night come alive. Kids laughing and playing among cows, people chatting in a lively tongue-clicking language, men singing and pounding on drums covered with animal hides . . .

It's late morning. I feel rested and energetic as I sit at the kitchen table to munch my cereal. Mum comes into the kitchen. "You okay?" she asks, holding my chin up and looking into my eyes. "I checked in on you a few times. You were so sound asleep I bet a hundred roaring lions wouldn't have been able to wake you."

I smile. "It's nothing, Mum. I guess I got carried away with this assignment. I was up most of the night."

"I've never known you to miss school, Thandi. Sure you're alright?"

She must really be worried to be talking to me this much. "Uh-huh. I'm going to take it easy today. Stay in my room and work on my assignment."

"What is this assignment?" she asks, shifting her eyes up to my hair. But before I can answer her question, she shakes her head and grumbles, "I'll never get used to that hairstyle of yours."

I flinch. "Remember that flyer I brought home from Mr. Roth? The one inviting parents to our World History presentations? It has to do with that."

I return to my room with a resolve to do a spectacular job on my ancestor presentation. This is going to be my chance to show my parents who it is they raised.

But as I settle down to begin work on the assignment, I develop an ache in my belly. I can't help thinking about the taunts of The Slugs, the comments kids have made about Africa, and the stupid questions I've been asked. Do I have the guts to ignore all that and proudly tell the class about my South African ancestry? What if they make fun of me? What if they think how backward and weird it all is?

With a groan, I fall on the floor. I wish I had the kind of self-confidence I saw in Salif. Slowly, I stand up and pace up and down my room.

My eyes fall on the library book I didn't get to yet. *I Write What I Like: A Selection of Steve Biko's Writings*. I flip through the book. Not an easy read, but it certainly grabs my interest. I find Biko's words not just inspiring, but very powerful. His big idea seems to be about building our self esteem. He says the first step toward our freedom from White domination is learning to like and be proud of who we, Black people, are. I read on, with growing excitement, and come to some lines that jump out at me:

"No wonder the African child learns to hate his heritage in his days at school. So negative is the image presented to him that he tends to find solace only in close identification to the white society."

Hmmm. I reread the paragraph. It's uncanny. He could have been describing me.

So, what is he suggesting? That we should not allow White people to try to make us think that White culture is better? I read on, thirsty for his wisdom and all the wonderful aspects of African culture that he describes and that I'd never paid attention to before. We have a lot to be proud of, Biko points out. He mentions, for example, our great capacity for friendships and how willingly we accept our fellow beings into our lives. He says that because of our attitudes about the earth and its riches, poverty never existed before the arrival of the White man in Africa. We shared everything and lived in villages as a community, helping each other. He describes the complexity of our traditional music and our dances. Like the effect of the first book I read last night, my soul is warmed by the many things I can feel proud of. This understanding of our African culture is what Steve Biko calls Black Consciousness.

I put the book down and stare at the ceiling, reflecting on what I just read. It's becoming much more clear to me what seeing the world with African eyes means. And I realize that looking at the world from an African point of view is not easy. Newspapers, movies, magazines always portray depressing stuff about Africa. This, perhaps, is one of the reasons why people freely put Africa down. So, instead of just taking it from people like Jennifer, Chrystal and Tess, I ought to defend the continent and its people, point out the many good things.

And that's exactly what Granny said in my dream. *It's up to you, Thandi. You make them understand.*

I go back to my desk, open a drawer, and pull out a picture frame. It's a photograph of my grandmother standing at the entrance to her house in Kheima. We used to visit her twice a month when we lived in Cape Town. Looking at her photograph makes me realize how much I miss her. I long for her voice, her smile, her exuberance.

I find a spot for the picture frame on my desk.

I know there's no stopping me now. I get on my bed, tuck my hands under my head, and concentrate on how I'm going to write my report and make my presentation.

Ideas flood my mind. Wouldn't it be terrific to actually have some Xhosa crafts and artifacts to show the class? And since singing and dancing are so essential to the Xhosa people, shouldn't they be included in my presentation, too?

Stacy's mum is the perfect person to help me out here. She has a mind-boggling collection of South African art, crafts, music, everything. I calculate what the time is in South Africa. It's eleven o'clock here in California. They are ten hours ahead of us, so it must be nine o'clock in the evening there. Stacy would still be awake.

I sneak out of my room and listen for Mum. I hear water running. Great. She's in the shower. I grab the phone and hurry back to my room.

As soon as I hear Stacy's familiar voice saying a very South African "Hell-oh," my heart does somersaults.

"Stacy, great to hear your voice."

"Hi stranger, how's America?"

"Hey, Stace, did you get the e-mail I sent you on Monday?"

"Yes, I did, you goose. Why, why did you relax your hair? *I* could have told you your parents would go ballistic."

"It's a long story," I mumble. "I can't talk about it now."

"Okay, but send me a photo with your next e-mail. I'm dying to see how you look."

"Sure. Hey, Stace, listen, I got you that leather jacket you wanted. My dad will mail it today."

"Fabulous," she squeals.

I explain the research report to her, and ask if I can speak to her mum.

Stacy's mum, Aunt Didi, lets out a whoop of joy when she hears my request. She gushes out ideas and names of the things she wants to send me. "And for music I'll send you an Amampondo CD. It's an old album, but wait till you hear them! I'm going to rush to the post office first thing in the morning and send the stuff by the fastest mail possible."

"Thanks, Aunt Didi. Remember, if there's anything you want from California, just let us know."

"Oh, Thandi, it makes me so happy that you are going to teach the Americans about traditional Xhosa life. You show them, girl."

I spend the rest of the day writing an outline for my report. There's so much information, it would be impossible to include all of it. I try to determine what important details should be included. Definitely music and dance. They are important to everything in the lives of the Xhosa people. How can I make them a part of my presentation? I'll play the tape Aunt Didi sends me . . .

I squeeze my eyes shut to sort out all the ideas buzzing through me. My thoughts drift to Kheima. I'm six years old and singing and dancing with the kids of the village. I've got to bring that real experience to the classroom. If I show the class a Xhosa dance—a proper one, not the jumping around I did with the kids—while the music is playing, it will have a greater impact on my audience than if I just tell them about it. But, that would be impossible since I don't know *any* African dance.

Wait. The Moore family will be here next Saturday evening for dinner. I could ask Salif and Tasha to teach me the dance they were doing when we visited them. Even though it would be a Masaai dance, it will give a similar impact. And surprise, surprise, I find myself looking forward to seeing the Moores again.

◊◊◊◊◊

The next day, Friday, between Algebra and World History classes, a sullen Jennifer heads for the outdoor basketball court, kicking loose rocks as she walks, her shiny hair bouncing on her neck. Chrystal and I are following close behind, totally against my will. Chrystal has her hand firmly on my elbow, pulling me toward Jennifer. Today is the first day that all three of us are back at school since Dad's presentation. Jennifer hasn't said a word to me all day. Fine by me. But Chrystal won't accept that I want space from them and she has been literally clinging to me.

Chrystal yells out to Jennifer. "Jennifer, you owe Thandi an apology."

"For what?" Jennifer demands, looking straight in front of her.

"For what we did during her dad's presentation." Chrystal is unusually serious.

"Well, she did it too!"

At that moment, Peter marches by, clutching a book, probably on his way to the library. Chrystal looks up and smiles at him. "Hi, Peter," she says in the friendliest of voices. Smiles at him and greets him! What in the world is going on?

Startled, he drops the book. "Um, uh, hey." He waves and grins back at Chrystal as he bends down to pick up his book.

I smile at him and say, "Hi, Peter." He looks away, ignoring me.

Jennifer glares at Chrystal, then turns around and storms away. Chrystal shrugs. "She'll get over it."

I shut my eyes aware only of the sinking feeling in my stomach. The e-mail I sent Peter hasn't changed anything. What will it take to make things right between us again?

Chapter 19

Aunt Didi's package arrives from South Africa a week after my phone call to her. On Thursday, soon after I get home from school the doorbell rings, and Mum answers. I hear a man say, "Ma'am, could you sign here, please?"

I dive into the living room. Mum gives me a puzzled look. "You have a package from South Africa."

I grab the neatly wrapped box. "Mum, this is for school. I'll explain everything on Tuesday." I bolt into my room, shut the door firmly, and rip open the box.

At the top is a letter with a purple ribbon tied around it. Immediately under it is a beaded necklace, big, broad, and boldly colorful. There's an African mask, carved out of wood, a little wooden drum brightly painted with animals engraved into the wood, a calendar with photographs of South African wildlife, a headdress decorated with feathers and beads, a CD labeled AMAMPONDO, and a small woven basket with ethnic designs in pale green and pink. Smaller gifts like our favorite South African candy bars and cookies are scattered in the box.

I read Stacy's letter, first quickly to get updated on all the news, then slowly, enjoying her artistic handwriting with its curves and curls, and giggling at her stories about the kids and teachers at Siyafunda.

I pick up the necklace and put it around my neck. A most un-California girl stares back at me from the mirror. I grimace. The necklace is so broad that it covers my entire chest. And because of the bright colors and intricate design, it looks like a costume piece. I immediately take the necklace off and throw it back into the box.

But questions about who I am pester me. Xhosa, Sotho, California girl, *Black people*, African, American.

My head is a swirl of confusion. I glance back into the box. The Amampondo CD stares back at me, daring me to listen to it. I stick it into my CD player and as soon as I hear the powerful rhythms and haunting sounds of the music, I'm yanked out of my muddled state. My entire body springs alive, like the desert when the rains finally come. And to my astonishment, I'm pining for the other world, for Kheima, and the Xhosa people, their singing and merriment, the cows in the fields, the bush . . .

Then, as if a spell is cast, I'm whisked away to a pretend world, a world where I can lose myself and feel free. I'm free to unleash my deepest desires. Desires so hidden that I often don't know what they are.

My neck and shoulders straighten as a defiant, daring, decisive feeling overpowers me. I will do my presentation and show the class who I really am.

Mum knocks on my door. I quickly turn off the music and stick my head out the door. "Got to do some shopping for Saturday evening," she says. "Could you come along?"

"Sure." I follow her to the car.

"Think Carol Moore and her kids would enjoy a South African-style barbecue?" Her tone is cool.

"A *braai*? Yah, great idea." A smile plays on my lips as I picture playing Salif and Tasha my new Amampondo CD. Funnier still is imagining their expressions when I ask them to teach me a Masaai dance.

As we drive to the store it isn't Tasha and Salif I think about. Instead, visions of the huge African sunset painting on Ms. Moore's wall flicker through my mind. How at home I felt at their house, surrounded by the arts and crafts so much like those of my native land.

At the store, Mum and I go up and down every aisle trying to find the kind of spices and ingredients we would use back home in Cape Town. We buy a bag of cornmeal to make *pap*, a porridge that we like to eat with barbecued meat. Mum selects the meat for barbecuing, and I gather ingredients for an egg and potato salad.

Mum is preoccupied as she drives us back home. She seems so far away from me emotionally. Normally we never run out of things to talk about.

Now, all I can sense is her anger at me. I run my fingers through my hair. And my eyes fill with tears. I glance up at Mum. Her short Afro neatly frames her scholarly face. She is beautiful.

◊◊◊◊◊

Saturday at six o'clock the doorbell rings. I bolt into the living room, praying Tasha and Salif didn't change their minds about coming. Ms. Moore has on her usual wide smile. "Hi," she gushes. Then she arches her brows and points to my hair. "Nice style."

Mum, dressed in a Zulu skirt, comes into the living room right at this moment. "Nice?" she hisses.

My eyes drop to the floor, then I look up and smile at Salif and Tasha. They twitch their lips slightly into what barely pass for smiles.

"Have you guys heard of the group Amampondo?" I ask them.

Salif frowns. "I think I might have a while ago."

"Come into my room. I'll play you a CD of theirs."

They exchange looks, shrug, and follow me.

Salif examines the label on the case as I insert the CD into the player. When the throbbing music comes on, Salif's face lights up.

"Oh, that is some amazing percussion!" he exclaims. He puts his ear closer to the speaker. "Hmmm, I think I hear a conga and, hmmm, can't tell what the other drums are. But, there must be at least three or four different kinds . . ."

Both Tasha and Salif move their upper bodies to the rhythm of the music. "Wow, that's pretty powerful music," Tasha says.

I turn down the volume a little. "Hey, do you think you two can teach me an African dance?"

Salif stares hard at me. "What?"

"Look, I've been doing a lot of thinking lately." My face gets hot. "And I, I guess I'm trying to figure out this whole 'being an African in America' business. Anyway, will you teach me?"

Salif presses his lips into a smile and nods with his eyes raised. "It's a tough one. African—Black, in America? I guess most of the brothers and sisters out there run around totally confused. I think the main thing is to go with how you feel here." He places a palm on his heart.

Tasha folds her arms and raises her brows at me. "Let me know when you've figured it out."

Salif moves my desk closer to the bed to make room. "I'm happy to help you. How about I teach you one especially for a young woman? First, we need volume." He turns up the music. Then he shouts, "Good, next you need to know a few basic moves. Foot, leg, and knee movements are really important. Arm movements are important too, but that part is easy."

About a half hour later I get the hang of some essential movements. "You're good, Thandi," Tasha says. "It comes naturally to you."

"Do you know what this dance is?" Salif asks.

Tasha laughs into her hands. "In the villages in Kenya when a young woman likes a man, she does this dance for him."

Peter's face floats into my mind. My smile fades away. How I long for his gentle smile and soothing voice. If he and I were living in a village in Africa, I would do this dance for him over and over until he forgave me.

Chapter 20

*O*n the second day of our ancestor presentations, I sit with my hands under my thighs, gripping the chair firmly as I watch the sequence of PowerPoint presentations. I feel sick. So much hinges on my presentation, the delivery of which is going to be done the old fashioned way. I didn't have the time to prepare anything that would involve a computer.

I've never before been so aware of the time as I am this Tuesday, March 6, 10:40 a.m. In five minutes, it will be my turn. A layer of perspiration covers my body. The door opens. Two parents leave, and Mum and Dad quietly enter. They wave at me and sit down on the chairs set up for parents.

"Thanks, Richard," Mr. Roth says, as he returns to his seat. "You did some wonderful research. Okay, Thandi, it's your turn." He looks at me and gives me an encouraging smile.

I walk up to the front with my box and set it on a desk against the wall. The first thing I do is put on the huge bead necklace. This triggers hooting. I feel myself weakening. I want to run away. I look at my parents. Dad's eyes are wide open. He's leaning forward, and smiling with his mouth open. Mum gives me the okay sign with both hands, and winks. That gives me strength.

"My ancestors were from the great continent of Africa, home to the Nile Civilization and some of the greatest marvels of humankind. I was born in South Africa. My mother is Xhosa and my father is Sotho. I have chosen to focus on the Xhosa today. Let me start by showing you some pictures of traditional Xhosa villages."

I get out the pictures and hold them up. "I'll pass these around so you can get a closer look. From these pictures you can see how the people in the villages live. They all have big smiles because well, they are surrounded by so much beauty."

Mum and Dad are mesmerized, chins cupped in hands, eyes fixed on me, their bodies leaning forward.

Encouraged by everyone's absorbed expressions, I breathe more freely. "The people of each village function like one big family. People grow vegetables, raise cows and sheep, and build their homes from what's around them. This is why the houses have thatched roofs and clay walls. The Xhosa are a people who live close to nature, respecting the riches of the land and sharing their wealth with each other. Greed, poverty, hunger, crime, and other problems of the modern world do not exist in these traditional villages. My grandmother still lives in such a village. It's where my mother grew up. I am so glad that I have the opportunity to experience the culture of my ancestors when we visit my grandma. These villages are disappearing and one day, not too far in the future, everyone will be living in built-up areas. It makes me sad to think that many aspects of Xhosa culture will be lost when this happens. But there are some aspects we can save, such as the crafts, the traditional music and dance."

I talk about the crafts and their significance, then I move on to brief descriptions of festivals and celebrations. "And I'm going to close my presentation with a dance performance."

With shaking knees, I get out my Amampondo CD and put it into the boom box. Everyone is silent, watching my every move. I mop the perspiration off my forehead with a tissue.

When the music comes on my skin tingles with excitement and my body automatically moves in rhythm. I hear Salif's dance instructions echoing in my head. I see Tasha laughing into her hands. I smile at Peter. His face looks tender, and my smile grows wider. My body and muscles relax as the tension slips away.

The tempo builds, absorbing all my attention. The audience fades into oblivion. I move my feet apart and shake my shoulders vigorously. The dance transports me away. Buena Vista and the western world are far in the distance. I'm in a time and place where the Xhosa and the Sotho are living traditionally. In *my* other world.

I throw my heart and soul into the music and

dance of my ancestors. My knees go up, I swing my hips, then stamp my feet. The dance suddenly takes on a new meaning. The fog of identity confusion is clearing up. I know and like who and what I am.

I'm all of it. Yes, all of it, and every aspect of me displays it to the world. My African hair in its natural state, Sotho lips, Xhosa nose, Cape Town accent, American clothes, and Californian love for ocean sports. And what better way to celebrate this wonderful combination that makes me who I am.

The music stops. Mum opens her purse, gets out a tissue, and wipes her eyes. Dad brushes a tear with the back of his hand. The wall between us collapses.

All the students cheer and applaud loudly.

I stride up to Mum and Dad. They hug and kiss me, proud smiles on their faces. "Thandi, what did I do to deserve such a wonderful daughter," Dad mumbles, taking my box from me and peeking inside.

"Ooh mama," Mum chirps, "Girl, you were stupendous!"

"Was I? Was I? Mum, I'm really sorry about my hair. It won't happen again. I'm with you on the natural look."

Mum smiles at me. "I know. I guess I did overreact. But, Thandi, if you lived through the history that we did, the pain, the humiliation, you'd understand."

I squeeze her hand. "I'm beginning to, Mum."

Mr. Roth calls up the next person.

"Are you staying for lunch?" I ask my folks.

They shake their heads. "No, I wish I could,

but I have to get back to the university," Dad says.

"I've got to go too," Mum says, "I'm meeting someone this afternoon."

I wave goodbye with the wonderful feeling that arises from knowing that things between me and my parents have changed—this time for the better.

◊◊◊◊◊

Lunch is a feast in Mr. Roth's classroom. A lot of parents prepared dishes from the countries of their ancestors. A beaming Chrystal walks toward me. She looks almost glamorous with her cool hairstyle and a new woolen top that drapes elegantly on her. "Thandi To-mah-to," Chrystal says, in her old, teasing voice. "You were awesome!"

So the dance didn't scare her away. She pulls me to the table of food, scoops up a creamy, gooey blob and piles it on my plate. "This is called *risotto bianco*, Thandi. Dad made it. It's yummy."

Dear faithful Chrystal. All it took was me to like and respect who I am, for her to respect me for who I am, too.

Chrystal and I pull our desks close together and settle down to enjoy our exotic meal. Along with the risotto, I have a tamale and a few sushi rolls. I look around the room for Peter and notice him sitting in the corner. Should I go up to him? I could use the excuse that I wanted to compliment him on his presentation.

"Thandi To-mah-to, what an awesome dance!" Chrystal chuckles light-heartedly. "Is that what you're doing for the talent show? It can be the two of us if you teach it to me."

This is such an unexpected suggestion that I just stare wordlessly at her.

She shrugs. "Just a thought. Jennifer's still upset. I don't think the band's going to happen…"

"Critical Chrystal, do you really mean that? You don't think it's a weird African thing?"

Her head drops. "Sorry for being mean."

"I forgive you. But listen, I think that's a great idea of yours about the dance. It's not what I was planning to do for the talent show, but maybe that's what I'll do. You and me."

Now it's her turn to be surprised. "Really?"

I nod. "Uh-huh, if you want, I can teach you the dance, and we can do it together."

"Look, Peter's sitting by himself," Chrystal points out. "Let's ask him to join us."

I dig my nails into my palms. My presentation helped smooth things out between my folks and me, but what about him?

Chrystal gestures for Peter to come and sit with us, then mutters, "That's really sad about his mom, huh?"

"What? Peter's mom? What about her?" I ask. My heart is racing. Peter is approaching our table.

"Later," she whispers as he appears.

Chrystal goes to get more food as Peter sits down. He looks at me with his bashful smile. "That was a wonderful presentation, Thandi."

"Thanks." I have to press my body down on my chair to prevent myself from jumping up and hugging him. "Yours was great too. You're good at connecting with your audience."

"Thanks." Our eyes lock.

Chrystal returns with a plate heaped with food. We stuff ourselves with as much as we can. Then Chrystal and I go out to the lower field for a break, and Peter goes off to the library where he volunteers.

"Chrystal, how do you know about Peter's mom?" We flop on our favorite bench under the Big Tree.

"Well, yesterday afternoon I was at the grocery store with my dad and we ran into Peter and his dad. So, I smiled at him and when our dads were out of earshot I told him I knew how hard it was not to have your mom around. He kind of shrugged as if it wasn't a big deal and said, 'I don't know my mom. She left when I was a baby.' I asked him if he knew where she was. He shook his head, saying his dad said something about drugs and alcohol being more important to her."

I feel a huge twinge of jealousy. Why did Peter tell *her* about his mom, and not me? "Where's your mom, Chrystal?" I ask.

She draws her lips in and folds her arms across her chest. "Colorado."

"For how long?"

"Forever, I think." She makes imaginary circles on the grass with her toes.

"Oh, so that's why you were so sad. When do you get to see her?"

She looks up at me with misty eyes. "Twice a year, during long vacations. Summer and Christmas."

"I'm sorry. That must be really hard. I would die if my mum lived away from home."

She sighs. "Well, it sucks. But at least my mom loves me and I can talk to her every day and we go on cool vacations and stuff. Look at Peter, he doesn't even know his mom."

Chrystal rubs her hands together and says, "Okay, teach me the dance."

Although we aren't able to play the CD on the field I have no problem teaching her the leg and arm movements and doing some practice steps. As we kick our knees up, I notice a shadow fall in front of us. I look up and see Jennifer staring at us.

"Want to join us?" I ask. "We're thinking of doing this dance at the talent show."

She frowns, shakes her head, and dashes away.

Chrystal lets out an impatient sigh. "What's her problem? Anyway, I hear things aren't working with Tyler, so I guess she's extra touchy."

It feels sad to let go of Jennifer, but I know now that she and I could never be true friends.

◊◊◊◊◊

I'm packing my backpack, getting ready to go home when Peter comes over to my locker. "Um, Thandi," he says in a hesitant voice. "I was wondering, you know the radio pen? Do you want to work on it this afternoon and see if we can have it ready for the talent show on Thursday?"

"What? Oh, the radio pen. Sure. Actually, even

if we succeed in getting it to work, I'm not going to enter it. There's something Chrystal and I are going to do together." Maybe I'm being silly. There is no way we'll win with the dance. But who cares.

He gives me a great big smile. "Want to come over to my place?"

"Actually, could you come to my house?" I'm sure I'm not grounded anymore. But I'm not taking anything for granted.

"Sure."

I grab my backpack and skip to the bike stands. Humming my favorite tune from the Amampondo CD, I bend down to undo the lock on my bike. Suddenly I hear giggles and shuffling feet very close to me. I look up. The Slugs are doing a mock African dance and screeching like morons.

Feeling like a hungry hawk in front of two pathetic slugs, I hold back the first words that come to my mind. Instead I fold my arms and sweep my eyes up and down them.

"I can only feel pity for people who have to pick on others for their fun. What dried-up minds you must have."

The Slugs exchange stunned looks.

"Whatever Sausage lips," Matt says under his breath, and the pair giggles like idiots, then turn around and walk away.

A light spring breeze caresses my face as I pedal down the path to my home. A monarch butterfly glides beside me, alighting briefly on golden California poppies along the way. Seagulls soar into the deep blue heavens. With my feet firmly on the pedals, I hold up my arms and try to embrace all of nature's miracles.

Dear Diary,

The most wonderful thing has happened to me here in Buena Vista, California. I see the world in a whole different way. Instead of trying to change the way other people look at me, I'm changing the way I look at myself. And yes, Mum is right about a diary. I simply have to write in complete detail how I found the path that led me to my African eyes.

About the Author

Ermila Moodley was born in Ladysmith, South Africa. A descendant of sugar cane plantation slave laborers, she grew up poor under the system of apartheid. Heavily influenced by South African civil rights leader Steve Biko and the Black Consciousness movement, she became involved in student protests and anti-apartheid political groups during high school and college. After earning a B.S. at the University of Durban-Westville in South Africa, she moved to California in 1987, and has been an elementary school teacher in the Santa Barbara area for the past fifteen years. *Path to My African Eyes* is her first published title with Just Us Books.